Costly Love
A Historical Novel

Linda A. Hatinen

© 2017 Linda A. Hatinen
All rights reserved.

ISBN: 1535104295
ISBN 13: 9781535104296

Dedication

This novel is dedicated in memory of my grandparents, Charles and Elina Soderburg on whose lives this novel is based.

Lynda Heinonen

Prologue: The Gift

My sister Amanda and I, like many sisters, have not been on the best of terms, especially lately, so I was surprised to receive a beautiful leather diary from her as a Christmas gift. I believe I receive insights about myself and life itself by writing, so why did she give me something she knew I would treasure when most days she will hardly speak to me? Though her motivation remains hidden, I will use my diary with great pleasure.

4 January 1887

Dear Diary,

My name is Elina Esaiasson. My father is Nils Esaiasson, and my mother was Anna Petersdotter. Mother was Father's second wife. I don't know how, but his first wife died. Anyway, I have one half-brother, Peter, who is at university and one older sister, Amanda. She is very prim and proper, smart, beautiful and used to be my best friend. She was born in 1866, and I was born on 14 October 1868. I have a younger brother Rudolf, who was born in 1877, and my younger sisters are Nathalia, born in 1871, Esther, born in 1873 and Josefina, born in 1883. Mother died giving birth to Josefina four year ago. I miss Mother's kindness and love, but the loss has been harder on Amanda. She can't seem to accept that Mother is gone or that we need to move on with our new situation. She does not like changes. Father is impatient with her, and that makes everything worse

We live on a farm named Ljungsjömåla. That's also the name of the road our farm is on, and the name of the small town that's close by. Father owns and runs our timber farm. I've heard people describe Father as brilliant, insightful, and ruthless. For whatever the reason, he is a very good businessman, running the largest timber operation in Blekinge, the small province in southwestern Sweden in which we live.

I've always loved our Swedish home. It is large, full of light and very airy. There are many fireplaces to keep us cozy in the long winters and twice as many windows to keep us cool in the much shorter summers. We have gardens all around the house, so I often can pick flowers to have inside. If I have a choice, I'll always live in a house like the one my parents have provided for me.

I grew up privileged, and now I realize it. Though Father has always been a hard taskmaster, he has been fair and generous to his children. At least that was true until my mother died. Since then he has become much more impatient and hard. It is as if when Mother died, the light went out of our home. I know he looks forward to the time when Amanda and I are married. I suspect he'd like to marry again but won't do so until we've left his home.

Father has hired additional domestic help and put Mrs. Stromberg in charge of our household. She is a kind woman as long as we do what she asks us to do. I don't have trouble with that, but sometimes Amanda becomes stubborn. She says she will not take orders from a servant.

Good night for now,

                        Elina

Part One

Ljungsjömåla, Sweden, 1887

"....Entreat me not to leave thee, or to return following after thee: for whither thou goes, I will go; and where thou lodgest, I will lodge: thy people will be my people, and thy God my God: Where thou diest, will I die, and there will I be buried...."

Ruth 1:16-17

1

New Thoughts

"Thou wilt shew me the path of life: In thy presence is fullness of joy; at thy right hand there are pleasures for evermore."

Psalms 16:11

The day is beautiful. The sun lights up the autumn trees, transforming them into gem-studded parasols. I enjoy the freshness of the air, the bright blue of the sky and the fall flowers I pass by on the way to my friend, Kirsten, in our small buggy, pulled by a single horse. In church this morning the priest announced the arrival of Kirsten's baby boy the previous week. I'm eager to see her and to present the baby with the soft yellow blanket I crocheted weeks ago in preparation for this blessed event.

Soon I turn into a driveway to a small red house where Kirsten and her husband Sven live. I was surprised a little over a year ago when the marriage had taken place and even more surprised when Kirsten told me that her father was allowing them to build a cottage on his land. Most landowners, including my father, refuse to divide their land, even to make room for a child's small home. The house is sweet but much more modest than anything I had expected Kirsten in which to live. But, as I hear frequently from Father, there are too many people and not enough land for them in Sweden. He's actually pleased that many young folks are migrating to America, but Kirsten has confided in me she would never leave her homeland.

I secure the horse to a sturdy bush and knock on the door. Kirsten meets me with a friendly greeting, including a hug. "Come in. I knew you'd come. Father Lindstrom must have announced the birth in church."

"He did," I reply. Kirsten has no domestic help, so I take off my bonnet and cape, placing them on a chair.

"Well, come on then. Follow me." We walk into a kitchen where Sven is holding his son.

"Would you like to hold him, Elina?" he asks.

"Of course," I say as I reach out for the little boy. "He's beautiful."

"We think so," Kirsten smiles. "Let's stay in here where it's warm. I'll put Lars in his cradle."

"Lars is a wonderful name, and you look so healthy and happy. Tell me everything, Kirsten."

Sven excuses himself, and we two friends sit in the kitchen watching little Lars sleep and talking about Kirsten's labor and delivery.

"I'm very happy for you, Kirsten, my friend. You seem to have made a good decision when you chose to marry Sven."

"Oh, I did, didn't I?" she laughs. "I love being married, and now the three of us are a real family. And what about you, Elina? Last I heard Arvid Johnsson was courting you."

"Don't even mention him, Kirsten. He's an old man, and I refuse to be his wife."

"Elina, you're shocking me. I always thought he was a fine gentleman."

"Yes, and he's even older than my father and already has buried two wives. He probably crushed them."

We laugh together though it's obviously funnier to Kirsten. "Seriously, I'd very much like to meet a man I could marry, but there aren't many eligible bachelors left in Sweden. Besides, Amanda isn't married either. We're both turning into old maids."

"Would that be so terrible?"

"Kirsten, I've always believed it is God's will that I would marry and have children."

"Well, dear Elina, maybe you'll be one of the many who leave for America. I've heard there are many more men than women there."

"That sounds way too desperate to me, but only God knows."

"Oops, it sounds as if my Lars is hungry. My milk came in just two days ago, so he and I are both learning about breast feeding, but feel free to stay."

As Kirsten settles little Lars to her breast, she looks intently at him. The two of them together remind me of a portrait.

For some reason, I suddenly feel as if I'm intruding, so I tell my friend it is time for me to return home. I say I'll see myself out and come again soon. Kirsten's only reply is a murmur, and I quickly don my cape and bonnet and leave the room, surprised and confused by the tears that begin to fill my eyes.

2

An Unexpected Meeting

"The LORD is my shepherd; I shall not want."

Psalms 23:1

The first half of the return trip home goes quickly as I think of Kirsten's happiness with her new life. I tend to be optimistic but still I can't see how my life could possibly have as happy a turn of events. After all, as the daughter of a large landowner, I can't marry just anyone. Father has told both Amanda and me that we need to choose husbands who will be suitable to help with the lumber business that has been in the family for generations. For the first time, I regret my status. I've had an easy life, a rich life, but I do not want to be denied marrying a man I love because of an obligation to my father. Oh well. I know no suitable men, so why am I fussing about a choice that doesn't exist?

As I make the turn toward home, I notice the mare is limping. Having been carefully taught to give good care to the animals upon which we all depend, I dutifully get off the buggy and began talking to Missy as I lift her front leg to check it. The shoe is slightly loose, but I can't see an injury. I pat Missy's nose and climb back on the buggy, but am startled by a deep voice asking "What's happened to your mare?"

"I can't say. I don't see any injury."

"Do you mind if I take a look?" he asks.

Instead of refusing him, as I probably should have, I answer, "Actually, I'd appreciate it. I don't want her to go lame."

He walks over from the side of the road where he must have been sitting and begins talking to the mare in a soothing tone. "Let's see what's happened, Missy." He gently lifts her leg and says, "It looks to me like she simply has some gravel under her shoe. It's a little loose. I'll see if I can remove it with my knife."

As I watch carefully, he slips a short knife blade under the shoe, releasing a few small stones. "There, that should do it."

"Thank you very much for your help. I have no money with me with which to pay you, but I'd like to give you something. Do you live near here?"

"I live wherever I can find work. I'm working on the Sorensson farm during harvest, but I visit my sister Olivia in Karlshamn each Sunday. I'm heading back from there now."

"The village of Karlshamn is on my way home. Perhaps I'll see you on the road again. I visit a friend here frequently. Thank you again."

"You're welcome, my lady. If you'd like, I'll leave my blade with you just in case your mare picks up more gravel. And do remember to have the shoe replaced."

"Thank you. And how can I get your knife back to you?"

"My sister's name is Olivia Jacobsson. She's a maid for Per Johnsson, a tailor in Karlshamn. But I stop right here each Sunday for a break before I walk the last eight miles. You could always find me here."

"That sounds good. I'll look for you next Sunday."

He smiles broadly, as he shakes my hand. "I look forward to seeing you again."

The rest of the trip home goes smoothly. When I bring the buggy to the stables, I tell Tomas, the farrier, about the loose shoe. With that done, I go inside, feeling surprisingly pleased with myself and my new acquaintance.

3

Daily Life

"And whatsoever ye do, do it heartily, as to the LORD, and not unto men."

Colossians 3:23

The days at Ljungsjömåla, the manor farm where I live with my father and siblings are filled with activities. Though of the upper class, Father is convinced his children, daughters and sons alike, should contribute to the farm, as well as being well educated. Amanda and I have both completed our secondary education. Amanda has no interest in attending university. I've told Father I would like to study literature, but he seems to think I can read books just as well at home. Father has decided to teach us how to manage the farm account books, while at the same time having Mrs. Stromberg continue to teach us domestic skills, including needlework, food preparation, child care and gardening.

My mornings start before dawn when I began milking the six dairy cows that provide milk for our family and my father's lumber crew. I know Father could have the hired help do the milking but suspect he wants us to know what the life of a farmer's wife would be, so we will choose a husband he feels better suited for us. I've only been assigned the milking for a month, but except for rising so early, I've grown fond of the cows and the peaceful task of milking. As I begin the chore the next morning, I think back to the young man I had met. I don't even know his name, but his surname probably is the same as his sister, Olivia Nikkolaisson. I toy with the idea of introducing myself to Olivia, but it would be awkward to explain why I was doing so. Instead I'll be patient and hope to see Mr. Nikkolaisson in a week.

In the meantime, I enthusiastically do the simple farm tasks I've been assigned plus helping with the cooking and cleaning, under the tutelage of Astrid, our cook and one of our domestic servants, Lila, and helping, Jonas, our gardener, tend the flower gardens, my favorite task. Following dinner, I usually have time to myself to read, walk, visit with my sister, or to concentrate on my needlework.

As Amanda and I sit with Mrs. Stromberg, while she knits we embroider pillow cases and Esther, Natalia and Josefina play with their dolls and Rudolph is outside.

Mrs. Stromberg interrupts the quiet, saying, "We need to start knitting lessons soon. Winter is a wonderful time to knit."

"Why do we need to learn to knit when you've already taught us to crochet, and for whom will you have us knit?" asks Amanda.

"Knitting is tighter and warmer than crocheting. There are always people to knit for: yourself, your babies, or your friends' babies. By the way, Elina, did Kirsten like the blanket you crocheted for her baby?"

"Mrs. Stromberg, I left in such a hurry when the baby started to cry in hunger, and I'd forgotten to give the gift to her earlier. I still have it, so I'd like to go again Sunday, if you don't mind."

"You silly girl to forget to give it to her. Amanda, why don't you go with your sister? It's good for both of you to learn about caring for babies, and there's nothing like a new mother to teach you."

"I'm not sure Amanda should go with. Kirsten seemed rather nervous about being a new mother. Could she wait a week or two?"

"That's thoughtful, Elina, and a very good idea. And now it's time for me to put my knitting aside and make sure Astrid has begun dinner."

"Elina, I'd like you to arrange flowers for the table. We're having guests at seven, so please dress for company."

"And who's coming tonight?" I asked.

"A few of your father's timber friends, and I believe one of them is a bachelor," she smiles.

"Oh, Mrs. Stromberg, no more match making. If we're to have husbands, God will provide them," says Amanda.

"There's nothing wrong with helping God. Just consider it a lesson in manners, if nothing else," she says as she leaves with our three younger sisters trailing behind her.

"Do you get the feeling Father is trying to get rid of us?" laughs Amanda.

"Amanda, I don't know how you can laugh. You should have seen how happy Kirsten and her husband are."

"So now you're eager for a husband?"

"Not really. I just know when the time comes I want to be the one to choose my husband, not have Father do it for me."

4

Merely a Lesson in Manners

"But my God shall supply all your need according to his riches in glory by Jesus Christ."

Philippians 4:19

A formal dinner in the farmhouse has become an occasion. Mother used to invite neighbors and acquaintances frequently, but that ritual came to an abrupt halt when Mother died. Amanda, and I, however, know that there are ulterior motives tonight and are not enthusiastic. Nevertheless, I make a beautiful arrangement of asters and chrysanthemums in one of Mother's vases and then set about preparing myself. We brush out each other's freshly shampooed hair and slip into our best frocks. As she admires herself in the mirror, Amanda adds a bit of color to her cheeks and lips and instructs me to do the same.

I look at my reflection in a long mirror: long light brown hair that has a bit of curl, deep blue eyes. I don't think of myself as beautiful but suppose I'm not exactly homely. My skin is clear, and my eyes are bright. I have to admit the bit of color I add lights up my face a bit. My frock is a beautiful blue satin, matching my eyes and showing off newly-acquired womanly curves. It is a modest dress, and I feel like a lady in it. Amanda has chosen her new green dress and asks me to fasten a locket around her neck just as Mrs. Stromberg walks through the door to inspect us.

"Well, you two look lovely." She smooths a few stray hairs, adjusts Amanda's neckline and then spots my hands, which are scratched from cutting flowers. "Elina, we can do nothing now, but please remember to treat your hands with lanolin each night. There's no reason for your hands to look like they belong to a scrubwoman."

"Yes, Mrs. Stromberg," I reply. "And is there a plan for this evening?"

"No, just be polite to your father's friends. Enjoy dinner, and eat more slowly than you usually do."

She had made it sound simple, but the meal itself is long and somewhat painful. Astrid has prepared a good meal: a broth with scallion slices, duck in some kind of buttery sauce, fluffy potatoes, roasted onions and parsnips, and delicious custard topped with lingonberries. It is fun to see Mother's china and crystal on the long, formal dining room table. The flowers are in the center with a pair of beeswax candles on each side. Astrid proudly serves each course she has prepared.

I have been placed between Erik Eriksson and Oskar Pedersson. Amanda sits across from me by Hjalmar Berg. Father introduces us to his friends, who almost immediately begin talking about the timber business. The dinner guests are concerned about the young people leaving Sweden and also the possibility of lumber being imported to Sweden from America.

"I hear there's virgin forest in much of the north," says Mr. Pedersson. "My cousin Axel wrote from Duluth that all he sees is virgin forests and water. He's started a lumber business since so many of the immigrants need housing. He seems to be doing well."

As the conversation goes on, Father attempts to include us in the conversation, telling the men Amanda and I have completed our secondary education years and presently are being taught housekeeping by Mrs. Stromberg and bookkeeping by himself. He actually looks proud as he talks about us.

The men smile at us, and Oskar asks me if I would show him the gardens. I look to Father for permission, and when he nods, I say, "Certainly. The flower gardens are my favorite part of the farm."

"Typical woman," chuckles one of the men, interested in the least useful part of a farm."

Following dinner, the men go to father's study to talk and smoke their pipes, but Mr. Pedersson offers his arm to me, and together we walk out to the garden. The August evening is pleasant, and I begin to name the flower varieties. He is plainly not interested in them, however, and finally says, "Elina, I want to learn more about you. You see, my wife died a few months ago, and to be frank, I need a wife to care for my three children."

Though I had suspected as much, I am shocked by his frankness and can only mumble, "How old are your children?"

"They're four, three, and six months."

"Did she—your wife I mean—die in childbirth?"

"Yes, she did, and I need to replace her."

The words seem very crude to me. How could he expect anyone to replace his wife? Had there been no love between them?

I walk in silence the rest of the way as Mr. Pedersson prattles on about his children, his house, and his business. I am relieved when he suggests we return inside. Not seeing my Father or Amanda, I excuse myself and go to my room, where I find Amanda waiting, curious and talkative. "Mrs. Stromberg said you made quite an impression on Mr. Pedersson. Did he tell you he wants to court you?" she asks.

"No, he did not, and if he had, I'd have told him I wasn't interested. What a boring man!"

"Mrs. Stromberg says he's very rich and even more ruthless than Father."

"So what, Amanda? What does that have to do with falling in love and marrying and living happily ever after?"

"I think you have been reading too many novels where everything is perfect."

"I don't expect everything to be forever wonderful, but I do know I'm going to marry someone I love—not some old wart who isn't a bit interested in me."

"But he *is* interested in you, Elina," Father says as he enters the room. He told me he was highly impressed with your obvious abilities and beauty."

"No, he's not. He just wants someone to take care of his children—and to warm his bed as quickly as possible. He actually said he needed to find someone *to replace his wife*. He gave me the creeps."

"Shame on you, Elina. You have much to learn about life and love. Since you've already changed into your nightgown, go to bed. We'll talk tomorrow."

As I lay in my bed, unable to fall asleep, I think about the evening and rue the fact I hadn't clearly told Mr. Pedersson I wasn't interested in "replacing his wife." He was so dull, however, he probably wouldn't have picked up on the emotion in my quoting of his crude words.

I retrieve the small knife Carl lent me from under my pillow, thinking how kind he had been to me and to my horse. If I were to marry anyone, I knew it would be someone who was kind. With that thought in mind, I kneel at my bed, saying my evening prayers, including seeking safety and health for the kind stranger whose knife I hold tightly in my hands.

5

The Stranger Becomes a Friend

"So God created man in his own image, in the image of God created he him; male and female created he them."

Genesis 1:27

Sunday has come, and I am filled with anticipation. I milk the cows with speed, eat a hearty breakfast and then groom myself with extra care and even add a bit of the color Amanda had shared with me earlier in the week. When she comes to the buggy, Mrs. Stromberg said, "You look lovely this morning, Elina. The color is very becoming."

We attend the Lutheran church services as a family as we always do. This week the priest announces the migration of several more young men to America. I have a difficult time concentrating on the sermon but know it is regarding the raising of children.

Sunday dinner is often a more formal meal, and today is no exception. While dining, Father leads us in his usual discussion of the Scripture lessons and sermon. Unusual for me, I have nothing to add to the discussion. Mrs. Stromberg notices my hurried eating and instructs me twice to slow down, an admonishment normally focused on the younger children. With the meal finally over, I ask whether I can take some of the left over buns to Kirsten, and Mrs. Stromberg agrees, preparing a basket with not only buns, but a crock of butter, and a crock of jam.

I gladly accept the basket and say I plan to spend the afternoon with Kirsten, and that this time I will not forget to give her the blanket I'd crocheted.

I happily leave the yard, wondering how I can claim some of the butter and jam for my new friend. The ride goes well, with no lameness in Missy. Kirsten is pleased to see me and seems much more relaxed with her baby. I hold him for a long time, enjoying the feeling of the warm bundle, believing once again I was meant to have children. We have coffee and a few of the buns with the butter and jam I'd brought. I had left two of the buns in the buggy but was delighted when Kirsten instructs me to take the crocks back home, so they won't be forgotten.

Kirsten appreciates the crocheted blanket and immediately wraps little Lars in it. I tell Kirsten I'll leave soon, so I'll be welcome again—maybe even the following Sunday. Kirsten says she'd love to see me again, and we exchange fond farewells.

I retrieve the buns I'd hidden away and tuck them in the basket with the half-filled crocks of butter and jam. Checking my pendant watch, I know I am slightly later than the first time I'd met "Mr. Nikolaisson," so I eagerly leave my friend's yard and turn hopefully towards home. I easily find the spot where he'd first appeared, and pull into a nearby opening where Missy can graze. I lift the bucket of water down for her also. That done, I take my basket and head over to the tree which marks the spot where I'd first seen him.

To my relief, before I even reach the tree, I hear the familiar deep voice say, "How good to see you again. I wasn't sure you'd come."

"Of course, I came. That's the least I could do to say thank you to someone who rescued me."

"You already said thank you, but I'll say you're welcome again. It was my pleasure to be of service. Is there anything else I can do to help you?"

"Just sit back down, and I will join you with some buns and butter and jam, and maybe we can learn a little about one another."

We spend the next hour together talking contentedly. He tells me his name is Carl Nikolaisson and that his father died when he was three. His mother remarried and died when he was fifteen, but he had been fortunate that his step-father and his new wife had allowed his sister and him to live with them for a few years.

I listen as he describes his life, never hearing even a trace of self-pity. I learn he has tried to enroll in the Swedish Army, but did not met some kind of requirement, so works on any farm that is hiring. He does say he is a good worker, so feels he will always be employed but will never be able to own land, if he remains in Sweden.

I am almost embarrassed to talk of my much easier life, but he listens so intently and asks such good questions that it is a pleasure to talk with him.

We learn we both have been raised in the church and feel God is an important part of our life and that he has plans for each of us. He is sorry that Sweden has a State church, believing it diminishes the meaning of faith and participation within a church. He has not been able to attend school nearly as long as I have, but continues educating himself by reading everything he can find. He's recently discovered an English author, Charles Dickens, and he raves about him.

We enjoy the buns with butter, and Carl says the jam is his dessert. He expresses appreciation of the small gift and then surprises me with a beautiful bouquet of flowers he'd picked while he'd been waiting.

When we agree it is time to leave, he walks me over to my horse and buggy. Once again, he pats Missy and gives her a handful of grass. The horse is grateful, but not as grateful as I am—for the wonderful afternoon. I put my hand in my pocket, retrieving Carl's knife. "Here you are, Carl."

"Why don't you keep it?"

"Are you sure you won't need it?"

"I believe I need you to have it until I can replace it with a more suitable gift," he shyly says.

"All right. Then I will say thank you, Carl, good-bye, and God be with you till we meet again."

"I will be here next Sunday, waiting for you, Elina."

He holds my hand as he helps me up onto the buggy, and then unties Missy from a tree, handing me the reins. To my pleasure, our hands touch once again, as he says, "Godspeed."

6

An Amazing Arrangement

> *"The LORD our God be with us, as he was with our fathers; may he not leave us or forsake us; that he may incline our hearts to him, to walk in all his ways and to keep his commandments, his statutes, and his ordinances, which he commanded our fathers."*
>
> *1 Kings 8: 57, 58*

Our innocent, short meetings continue through the remainder of the fall. I had never felt as comfortable talking with anyone as I did with Carl. As the weather begins to get colder, we both knew our enjoyable meetings will have to end.

In the way that small happenings can impact much of someone's life, an occurrence in the autumn months changes the direction in which Charles' and my lives are headed. Knowing that Father had recently lost several workers to America, I simply ask Charles if he would consider looking for work at Ljungsjömåla.

He does not reply, but later that week, at dinner, when Father mentions his shortage of good workers, I casually remark that a man had helped me on the road, and I know he is looking for work. After his tirade against my allowing a complete stranger to assist me, Father says to go ahead and tell him to come see him.

Two weeks later Father announces he's hired three new men, one of which is Carl Nikolaisson. I can barely control my excitement and am relieved when no one notices my warm cheeks that must have been bright red.

The next day Father asks all of us to come out to the yard to meet the new men, a tradition he'd begun years earlier. The family members are introduced and then the men's names are given. When Carl is introduced, I say, "This, family, is the kind man who rescued me on one of my trips to see Kirsten." I knew I would not admit I had met him on a weekly basis but did not want anyone to wonder how we were "somewhat" acquainted.

I was shocked when later that day after bookkeeping lessons, Father said, "So how often did you see Nikolaisson on the road?"

"He visited his sister at Karlshamn about the same time I went to see Kirsten, so I saw him almost weekly and talked with him a few times."

"And nothing inappropriate transpired?" he asked.

"No Father. He was a complete gentleman, and I was a lady. You have raised me well."

"Elina, many people would forbid you from interacting with anyone in the lower class, but I believe our world is changing, and I don't fully agree with those restrictions. However, don't allow your heart to be reckless. You have to realize all you would lose."

"I appreciate that understanding, Father, but please do not expect me to marry one of your widower friends."

"Very well, Elina. I've always known you to be independent but sensible. Feel free to talk with Mr. Nikolaisson but only if Mrs. Stromberg, Amanda, or I are in your presence."

His permission to let me continue in the friendship was not only amazing but a huge relief. "May he come to the flower gardens if others are around?" I ask.

"Yes, and I will tell him myself that he is allowed to do so."

7

A Friendship Deepens

"A friend loves at all times…"

Proverbs 17:17

Father and I were both true to our word. I was greatly relieved not to be deceptive and found a great joy in knowing I would see Carl regularly and talk with him at least a couple times a week. As the fall grew colder, Father extended his permission for garden walks while Mrs. Stromberg sat inside sewing as she chaperoned.

The garden, in November, was drab to most people, but to Charles and to me it was beautiful. Carl was interested in everything—even the flower gardens. He was surprisingly knowledgeable about the names of varieties and asks questions about the few he does not recognize.

He was somewhat intimidated by the splendor in which I live, but I was quick to remind him that God sees people's hearts, not the trappings they own. Carl said, "Yes, that's true, but to people, the trappings matter."

"Well, maybe they shouldn't," was my reply. And then the topic changes to literature which we both enjoy. I learn that the only books he has ever owned are his confirmation Bible and Luther's catechism. I think of my father's vast library in the house and even my own bedroom shelf filled with books. What contrasting lives we've lived!

Later I ask Father if I may give some of my books to the men in the bunkhouse, and he answers, "Yes, you may give them to Carl, but do not also give him your heart with them."

December and January are usually bitterly cold and snowy in Sweden, and even I know the garden walks will have to temporarily end. I do manage to buy two Swedish copies of <u>A Christmas Carol</u> by the English writer of which Carl has talked, Charles Dickens. I wrap one for Carl and inscribe it "To my dear friend, Carl, from Elina". After reading the other copy, I eagerly wait to discuss it with Carl.

As Christmas preparations are underway, Father announces that all but four of his men are returning to their families to celebrate Christmas, and he wants to invite the remaining four for Christmas Eve dinner in the manor. This was a practice I'd grown up with. After Mother's death, Father hadn't continued doing so, but I was pleased Father was reinstating the practice. I didn't doubt for a moment that Carl was one of the men who was staying. After all, he really has no home to which to return.

For the first time in five years, our house is decorated with a beautiful spruce tree and tree boughs and candles are at every window. Our dining room looks extra festive to me with the candles, beautiful lace trimmed linens and Mother's best china and crystal. Mrs. Stromberg has made place cards, and I am thrilled to learn Carl will be seated next to me. Small, wrapped gifts are at each person's plate, adding to the festivity.

We girls all wear our green velvet skirts with white lacy shifts and our hair is pulled back with ribbons. Father, Peter, and even little Rudolf are in cutaway suits. Father ushers in the four workmen, and though they are rough looking, their clothes are neat, and their hair and skin shine with cleanliness. I know I will always remember this night and believe the workmen will also.

After we sing grace, Father warmly welcomes the four men, and everyone begins helping themselves to food from the ample array of traditional food being served: lutefisk with cream sauce and butter, meatballs, boiled potatoes, boiled carrots, lingonberries, a variety of breads and rice pudding with scrumptious cookies for dessert.

Carl asks questions quietly of me, and I answer them with joy. He admires the beauty of our home and the abundance of food. After we've eaten, everyone opens the gift in front of them: warm leather mitts for the workmen, and books for the family members. Amanda, an accomplished pianist, plays Christmas carols on the piano, and the family sings with her.

Father, noticing the men are not participating, politely tells them they should feel free to leave anytime, but that they are all invited to accompany us to church services on the wagons we'll be taking.

The men thank for their gifts and meal, and Carl and the farrier, Tomas, say they would like to go to church with us.

And so we all get bundled in coats and capes and fill the wagons. There are fur robes and blankets to keep us warm, and we sing on the way to church. Amanda and I are put in charge of the little girls and Rudolf, who are fascinated by Carl and Tomas' presence and pepper them with questions. When we arrive at the candlelit church, Tomas says he will stay with the horses, and for an awkward moment I believe Carl will stay outside also, but instead he follows us inside. Carl stops and sits down in a back pew while my family walks to the front of the church to our usual spot.

Greetings are exchanged with many neighbors and acquaintances until the pipe organ comes to life, and the congregation becomes quiet. The children fall asleep while the priest preaches the Good News of the Gospel, and when the town bell rings twelve times, we all greet one another with "God Jul", the Swedish Christmas greeting, and happily leave the church.

Tomas and Carl have brought the wagons close to the church doors, waiting in line like many other groomsmen are doing. Father thanks them for their thoughtfulness, and if I saw correctly, slips a coin into each of the man's hands.

Back home, the wagons bring us right to the door. Before I lose my nerve, I hand to Carl the wrapped book I'd purchased. Much to my surprise, he takes a small bag from his pocket and hands it to me. We exchange thanks and Christmas greetings, and Carl quickly kisses my cheek, and then Mrs. Stromberg asks me to help with the young girls by taking Nathalia and Josephina to their beds. They are so sleepy they can barely walk.

I help them undress and tuck them in, and finally in the privacy of Amanda's and my room open the small package Carl has given me. I find a beautiful wooden bird which I am sure he has carved. Included is a short note in beautiful handwriting:

> "Merry Christmas to my dear friend, Elina. May this bird I carved for you remind you of my fondness for you each time you see it.
> Yours truly,
> Carl"

The carefully and warmly written note pleases me as much, if not more, than the beautifully carved bird, which I carefully position on my bedside table.

Amanda comes in as I am putting away my clothing. For reasons I don't fully understand, I hope Amanda will not spot the gift I treasure, but she does, asking, "What is that?"

"It's a bird Carl carved for me. Isn't it beautiful?"

"I suppose it is—if you like plain, wooden birds. By the way, I heard Father and Mrs. Stromberg talking. Mrs. Stromberg thinks it was a mistake for Father to have invited the men for our Christmas Eve dinner. She thinks you're getting too close to Carl. Did he truly kiss you?"

I feel my cheeks grow hot but ignoring her question dare to ask, "And what did Father say?"

"He said you'd get over it. You aren't foolish enough to fall in love with a pauper."

I am so angry I cannot reply. It had never entered my mind that I was falling in love or that Carl is a pauper. I was simply enjoying a lovely friendship—my first friendship with a man. It wasn't as if he were courting me, but I do think of him with tender feelings, and his note, gift, and kiss have touched me deeply. I turn my back to Amanda as I kneel at my bed, asking my Heavenly Father to help me to understand my feelings and to keep Carl safe.

As I climb into bed, I realize it is the first time in my memory I had not prayed for each of my family members, and I return to my knees to do so.

Amanda notices and says, "You must have a lot to pray about."

I ignore my sister, climb back into bed and pull my beautiful lace-edged linen sheets and soft eider quilts over myself. Once again I turn my back on my sister, who seems to be in no hurry to fall asleep.

8

New Routines

"If you fulfil the royal law, according to the scripture, 'You shall love your neighbor as yourself,' you do well. But if you show partiality, you commit sin, and are convicted by the law as transgressors. For whoever keeps the whole law but fails in one point has become guilty of all of it."

James 1:8-10

The beautiful Christmas season passes, and the cold winds of January howl through the farm. My father has not spoken to me of Carl, nor has he provided any occasions where we can be together.

I know my feelings towards Carl have changed, but I do not know how to describe them. I wish Mother were alive so I could talk to her. Amanda used to be my confidante, but her remarks of late have hurt me, as she makes no attempt to hide her feelings that Carl is not good enough for me. I believe she is looking out for my benefit, and probably mirrors the opinion of most of our social strata, but I wish she would get rid of her class prejudice. Just because we've been raised as elite, are we to look down at everyone else? I don't believe that's right, and I certainly don't believe it's Christian.

I refuse to invite any more criticism, so, instead, I keep busy, applying my homemaking instruction from Mrs. Stromberg, Astrid, and Lila, more seriously than previously. I also welcome my bookkeeping instruction from Father, and even he says I am making good progress.

In my free time, I read profusely, dream of a young man with curly black hair and write in my diary in an attempt to clarify my thoughts:

> *10 January 1888*
> *Dear Diary,*
>
> *I did not know my emotions could be so complicated. Maybe it's that I'm at an age when I want to be married or maybe I've been influenced by my friend Kirsten's happiness with her husband and baby. I don't know. What I do know is that I believe Carl is a good man. He is kind and gentle and very interesting to talk with. Father has pointed out very clearly that he is a pauper, and he won't approve of anything beyond a friendship with him. But I wonder if God put him in my path. If so, then wouldn't He want me to fall in love with him? I look at the bird Carl carved for me and know it was made with love. Nothing else could have made it so beautiful. I have not talked with Carl since Christmas and can hardly wait to do so once again.*
> *Good night for now,*
> *Elina*

Winter turns into spring, and opportunities for walks with Carl resume. I find we both enjoyed <u>A Christmas Carol</u>, as we discuss it at length. I had received other novels as Christmas gifts, and instead of adding them to my growing collection after I've read them, I give them to Carl. He is extremely appreciative, telling me that to him each book is a treasure.

Carl has mentioned America during our summer talks, but now he begins to talk seriously about leaving Sweden. I do not know if that leaves a chance for a friendship, but one afternoon he says, "There is no future for you and me to be together here. I would never want you to be thought of poorly by your peers."

At that moment, I did not have the opportunity to ask him to clarify what he meant since my sister Nathalia needed me, and for the following two weeks, which seem endless, there are no walks since the harvesting of wood is underway in earnest, and the men stay in the forest.

Father allows a work break from Good Friday through Easter Monday, and once again most of the men, including Carl, to my surprise, leave to be with family. On Easter Monday Father calls me to the porch, where I find Carl waiting for me.

"Elina, I believe Carl has some news for you. Feel free to visit with him for a while."

It is a strange permission, but I immediately understand when Carl says, "I'm sorry to have not given you more warning. I spent Easter with my sister and saying farewell to my step-parents. I'm leaving for America on May twenty-second. I've given notice to your father, but I needed to talk with you. I told your father I plan to save money to buy the passage for the girl I hope to marry. What I didn't tell him is that girl is you."

My shock at his words must have been visible to Carl, as he says, "I know that sounds presumptuous. I've withheld much of how I feel about you. I only ask for now that you allow me to write to you, and if you possibly learn to love me, then I will ask you to give me the gift of your hand in marriage."

"Carl, I'm ever so fond of you, but you have surprised me. Of course, I would like for you to write to me, and I will answer. Let us just wait to see what our hearts tell us."

"Thank you, Elina. You have given me a wonderful hope, and I must tell you there is no other woman I have ever thought of in the way I think of you. And now I must go, or I will take you in my arms, and your father will come out here with a shotgun in his hands."

With that he leaves for the bunkhouse, and my eyes overflow with the tears I don't know how to explain. As I go inside, Father sees my tears and says, "It looks as if Carl told you he'll be leaving for America, and that he has a girl to whom he's engaged. I hope he hasn't been leading you on."

I manage to say, "No, he's been very honest, but I will miss him. I've enjoyed getting to know him."

9

Letters

"Let such people understand that what we say by letter when absent, we do when present."

2 Cor. 10:11

I never saw him again—at least not in Sweden. He left six weeks later while I was in town with Mrs. Stromberg and Amanda. While gone, it dawns on me that Father had planned the trip as a diversion for me. He must believe I am brokenhearted since in his eyes I've been jilted. I don't correct his misconception simply because I am still trying to understand Carl's pronouncement of love and desire to marry me. I am thankful he has not pressed me for an answer because I do not know what I would say.

The days go on with spring progressing to an early summer. As always, the longer days, along with greenery and blossoms make the entire population feel much more optimistic. On a day in late June Amanda tells me I have a letter from America. I spot the letter on the hall table addressed to me and from Charles Soderberg, a name I don't even know. The beautiful, flowing penmanship looks somewhat familiar, but I cannot identify it.

> *15 June, 1888*
> *My dear friend Elina,*
> I have reached America after a long, fascinating trip across the enormous Atlantic Ocean. I was amazed by how much water there is. The steamship I was on went directly to Canada. From there I took a train to Duluth, Minnesota, the home of many Swedish immigrants. I am living in a boarding house run by a Swedish widow who seems to have a soft spot for me. You don't have to worry though; she's 50 years old and treats me like her son. She's given me lots of tips and even told me to use her name for a job reference. That worked out well since I was hired at the second place I inquired-- as a dock worker, loading and unloading ships. It's hard manual work but pays very well. By the way, Mrs. Gundersson, my landlord, is the sister-in-law of the owner of the loading business where I'm working. I feel that God definitely has a plan for me (and I hope and pray it includes you).
>
> *With affection from your*
> *American friend,*
> *Carl*

I answer the letter the next day, wondering whether Carl is using an alias to prevent my father from knowing we are corresponding. Whatever the reason, I address my return letter carefully to the strange name and address on the envelope's return.

> *10 July 1888*
> *My dear American friend,*
> I was ever so pleased to receive a letter from you and to know that you are safe and doing well. To have a place to stay and a good-paying job is

> wonderful. I looked at a map and found Duluth right on the tip of a huge lake. It must be beautiful where you are. I will write more when you explain the name you used on your return address. Am I truly writing to Carl or to someone named Charles Soderberg I've never met?
>
> > Sincerely,
> > Elina Esaiasson

I put my letter with the mail to be posted, and when Father asks who Charles Soderberg is, I answer vaguely that he is an old friend. Father appears puzzled with the answer but asks nothing more.

The next few weeks are agonizing for me. I remain puzzled over the Charles Soderberg name and am concerned Carl will not receive the note I'd written, but finally another letter addressed exactly the same and with the same return name and address arrives.

> 5 August, 1888
> My dear Elina,
>
> > I am so sorry to have alarmed you with my new name. When boarding the ship in Liverpool, I was asked what name I wanted. To quote the man recording the names, "Now don't use a name no one but a Swede knows how to pronounce let alone spell." As quickly as I could I came up with Charles Soderberg. Charles after the wonderful author Charles Dickens and Soderberg, Swedish for south mountain, of course, indicating where I was born and therefore honoring my Swedish roots. I hope the name is satisfactory to you since I'd like you to share it some-time in the future.
> >
> > I am pleased you checked out a map. Isn't it amazing to see how far I've traveled? Lake Superior is beautiful. Duluth, itself, is a very young city and somewhat primitive, but as I see buildings going up, I know it will be beautiful in the future. Currently, there is a big shortage of housing, and what is being built for immigrants is especially crude.
> >
> > Work goes fine. I'm getting to know the men I work with. Most of the men are from Sweden and Finland. I've learned those two countries have a reputation for sending hard workers to America. They're a rough crowd prone to drinking and visiting the houses of ill repute, but I am not

tempted by those vices. Instead I'm saving every dollar I earn, except of course to pay for my room and board. I will need to purchase a new shirt and pants soon, as mine are wearing out, but that doesn't surprise me. Mrs. Gundersson said she'll help me find those items at a good price. She knows I'm saving to pay for your passage.

Forgive me for not explaining my name change. I've gotten so used to it, I've almost forgotten my old name, so

With apologies and deepest admiration,
Charles Soderberg

26 August, 1888
My dear Charles,

Now that you've explained it, I consider Charles Soderberg a perfectly wonderful name. Until I understood, it felt as if you'd disappeared. It was very troubling to me.

My sister Amanda has suddenly decided she wants to go to America to become a teacher. I was very surprised when she made her announcement at dinner this week. Unfortunately, Father was not pleased with her, especially since he's been pressuring her to choose an older man to marry or to continue with her education. She, however, says she will not do so. Do you think it would be work out if she also lived in Duluth?

Waiting to hear from you,
Elina

I realize my life is suddenly beginning to revolve around the letters I receive and write. Everything else is unimportant to me. I long to tell my father about Charles, knowing that being deceitful with him is wrong. I comfort myself, remembering I have never actually lied. Yet, I know I am doing wrong and confess my sin to my Heavenly Father.

14 September, 1888
My dear Elina,

Unless I read it incorrectly, your last letter seemed to indicate you expect to migrate to America. Does that mean you are going to agree to my proposal? I am trying hard not to pressure you, but it is on my mind continually. Please write soon, so I am no longer in suspense.

With greatest hope,
Charles

15 September, 1888
Dearest Elina,

I am sorry if I seemed too eager in the letter I wrote to you yesterday. If I could, I would have reached into the Post Office slot to retrieve it. I'm afraid I was very rude and presumptuous. It is just that when I read your letter, I became so happy that I lost my sensibilities. I await your forgiveness—and your answer.

With apologies,
Charles

7 October, 1888
My dear Charles,

I have read your last two letters repeatedly. I have come to understand that your happiness is in my hands. With that realization, I can only say that I would be honored to be your wife. I know we must wait until you've saved enough money for my passage, but I am no longer fearful or even reluctant to make a commitment to you. I have prayed for guidance from our Heavenly Father, and I have realized that it is not only His will that I marry you, but that He put you in my life. How else can I explain meeting you on the road?

I would like to tell my Father of our decision but will wait until I hear from you to make certain we are both sure of our plans.

My love,
Elina

29 October, 1888
My dear Elina,

I feared your letter would never come, but now that it has arrived I am beyond happiness. That you desire to speak to your father makes me feel you are sure of your heart. It would not surprise me if he tries to dissuade *you, but I pray that you have strength to resist him. If you want Amanda to come to Duluth, tell her to do so. I know I will never see my sister again, but if you can live close to yours and you want to, then encourage her to come also. Just so we're clear I will not be able to send money for her passage because I know we will want to have a house built as soon as possible. When I left Sweden, I believed it would take me three years to purchase your passage, but if nothing goes wrong, I should have the money in two years. I want you to become my wife in 1890!*

With greatest happiness,
Yours, Charles

20 November, 1888
My dear Charles,

    You are a kind and good man. I wait for your letters and marvel when they arrive. Just think they come across the ocean! And you write so beautifully.

    I had not thought of how long it would take for you to save money for my passage, and I'm afraid you're denying yourself too much. However, 1890 sounds like a long time from now, and I don't want to wait longer, so I say thank you for living frugally, and one day in 1890 and from then on I hope you will be able to tell me your sacrifice was worth it.

With all my love,
Elina

14 December, 1888
My dear Elina,

    We have been hit with a huge snowstorm, so everyone working on the docks was sent home. Truly, the whole city seems to be shut down. Yesterday Mrs. Gundersson had a small St. Lucia Day celebration here with cardamom bread. It was very simple, but tasted like home.

    Since I have lots of time today, I thought I'd tell you a little more about my life. I get up in the dark each day, get dressed and go to the dining room for breakfast, which is almost always porridge with milk, bread and cheese and strong coffee. By the way I spent a dollar on a pocket watch since writing last. With the long, dark nights I needed a reliable timepiece so I'm not late for work. Anyway, Mrs. Gundersson packs a lunch for me and a few other fellows for an extra dollar a week. That seems to be a reasonable price and keeps me from stopping at a shop where lunch would be closer to a dollar each day. Anyway I work till darkness approaches, and then go back to the boarding house for a supper of soup, bread and butter and sometimes cheese. Mrs. G. serves fruit a couple times a week also.

If I'm not too tired, I spend my evening reading. There's a shelf of books in the dining hall, and I've made good use of them. I've even found more books by Charles Dickens. He has much to say about the different classes of people and seems to have a soft spot for the lower class of which I know I'm a part. On Sunday, my one day off, I usually take a long walk, just to see what is here. There are a handful of beautiful buildings, and more being built. The Swedes mostly seem to have settled in one area called Swede Hill. I've talked to some of the folks there, and they're nice enough, but the houses are poorly made. We might have to settle for such a place at first, but if God's willing, I'd like to have a farm. That seems to be an ideal place to raise children. I know we haven't talked about it, but I hope we can have several children. I suppose I want to make up for being raised as an only child until Olivia was born.

I have found a Lutheran Church here and am attending regularly. It's called Bethany Lutheran Church. The pastor (by the way the clergy here are called pastors not priests) is a good man. I've already told him about you, and that we are engaged. He's offered to marry us! When I told him of my plans to own a dairy farm, he told me in the spring he'd like to show me an area settled by Swedes called Midway Township. He's told me it's close to Duluth, but on top of the hills I can see. Pastor told me the land flattens out and has good grazing. I'm told there's a group of Swedish worshipers there also.

I've started English classes that the pastor teaches. I want to master the English language, and I have a small start.

I've probably rambled on too much. It is amazing to think we'll be able to talk to each other every day in 1890. I await that time.

With my love,
Charles

4 January, 1889
My dear Charles,

Your long letter arrived, and it was my very favorite Christmas gift. Before I forget, I hope you had a Merry Christmas and will have a Happy New Year. Now that it is 1889, we can say we are going to be married next year!

I told my father that we are engaged. Surprisingly, he was not angry—just surprised. Father is convinced that moving to America is a good decision. He talks often about the shortage of land and opportunities in Sweden, and he agrees with you that a man needs to own land. He also said that for the short time you worked here, he could tell you were an ambitious and responsible man. He did say it is very difficult to know he will not see me married or meet his American grandchildren. On the other hand, he's asked one of his workmen to build a traveling trunk that he says we will all fill with things you and I will need in our home.

I also asked for his forgiveness for my deceptiveness. He was very merciful, and I feel much better.

Filled with love,
Elina

27 February, 1889

My dear Elina,

I mailed a letter to your father, asking for permission to marry you, and he has already given me his consent in the form of a telegram, the first I've ever received. My hands shook when I opened it, thinking he was not allowing you to come to me. Instead, he was very cordial, and I am very pleased by his kindness. I must admit it was Mrs. Gundersson who suggested I write a letter to him, and once again she has revealed her wisdom and kindness to me. She told me that when the time comes she will help us to find a house and furniture for it.

More good news, my boss has given me a small raise. 1889 has started out very well for both of us.

With love and gratitude,
Charles

9

Preparations

"Then the LORD God said, 'It is not good that the man should be alone; I will make him a helper fit for him.'"

Genesis 2:18

The letters continue to come very regularly, and I answer just as regularly. Each one I receive I think of as a gift to be savored. I have begun to anticipate marrying Charles in May or June of 1890. I know that Charles is working hard in America to earn money and saving every penny that is possible to save. I expect to be leaving Sweden in May.

In the meantime, my father is equipping me in every way he feels he can. My instructions in homemaking and child raising have become a greater priority to me because I know I will be applying those skills next year in America. While instruction is being given by Mrs. Stromberg, Father has had a large travel trunk made out of fine oak lumber. It is two meters wide, a meter deep, and a meter and a half tall. It has a rounded lid that not only latches but has a sturdy lock. On each end there's an iron handle, making it easier to carry, but I can tell that, handles or not, it will require two or more men to carry it.

In the trunk I've packed practical woolen knit socks that are fruits of my labors. Together Mrs. Stromberg, Amanda and I work on a woolen patchwork quilt that we will have ready prior to my departure. Pillowcases, trimmed with embroidery and tatting have appeared in the trunk along with dresser scarves and beautiful linen tablecloths and napkins. Father hired a seamstress to make skirts, shirts, a fine woolen coat and cape as well as silk under garments for me. He has asked our gardener to accumulate a small supply of vegetable seeds, and I've begun collecting herbal and flower seeds. Under Mrs. Stromberg's direction, Astrid, the family cook, packaged spices that might be difficult to obtain in America as well as carefully writing down recipes the family favors. I even wrote down directions for the many soups she makes—even though she had never before thought a recipe would be needed to make them.

It amazes me that the items in the trunk seem to grow each week. One day I saw Father put a beautiful wooden clock inside, and the next day I watched him add a few of his small tools. From his letters, I know Charles is learning English from the Lutheran pastor, who has started teaching classes on Sunday nights. He believes learning the English language is an important step for immigrants to become part of their new home. I found a small pamphlet containing English phrases, and I've been practicing them. I have so little to do while it seems that Charles' life is one of hard work and very few pleasures. It amazes me that he never complains, and I promise myself I will do my best to make life easier for him as soon as I can.

Mrs. Stromberg, who has asked me to call her Tilly, encouraged me to ask my friend Kirsten about childbirth and breast feeding. When Tilly seemed dissatisfied with what I told her Kirsten had relayed, she arranged for me to spend a few days with a local midwife who is her friend. When I returned home from my stay with the midwife, I had much to talk over with Tilly, who confided that when she was married she knew nothing about conceiving or delivering babies and did not want me to enter marriage as unprepared as she was, especially without relatives nearby. As we have talked about marriage, including the marriage bed, I have become very close to her, thinking of her as a second mother. Her contribution to the trunk is a bundle of nappies, baby clothing, and blankets. She hugged me, as she now does frequently, after she placed the items in the trunk.

Father, as a true businessman, is going over his ledgers with me. He's been teaching me bookkeeping for months, but now he even goes into his business philosophy on how to keep a farm profitable, and where and when to take financial shortcuts. The one thing he emphasizes most is not to go into debt for anything, with the exception of the purchase of land. He's even added a blank ledger book to the trunk, telling me to use it no matter how small a farm with which we start.

And then, finally, on April 14, 1890, along with a letter from Charles come three tickets, one from Gothenburg to Hull, England; one from Hull to Montreal, Canada and a train ticket from Montreal to Duluth, Minnesota, United States of America. I am so excited I can barely contain myself, telling everyone on the farm that the tickets have arrived. I really am going to become Charles' wife.

10

Across the Ocean

"If I take the wings of the morning and dwell in the uttermost parts of the sea, even there thy hand shall lead me, and thy right hand shall hold me."

Psalms 139: 9, 10

On May 16, 1890 my father, my sister Amanda, Tilly and I leave Ljungsjömåla in our wagon, along with the large trunk filled by my family, traveling for Gothenburg, a port northwest of home from which I will travel to England and then take a steamship to North America. Most of the time we travel, Tilly and I talk quietly, and I weep softly. Father and Amanda sit across from us having their own conversation which seems very stilted as Amanda is in a bad mood.

The trip finally ends as I check to make sure I have my traveling papers issued by our parish priest as well as the tickets sent by my soon-to-be husband.

Father sent Tilly and Amanda off to find lunch for us. He is very familiar with the Gothenburg dock area and suggests they look for fish to eat. He points out there are picnic tables close to the ship I will be taking, the Orion, and says they should bring the food there. Father gives Tomas, the groom, money for his own lunch and to have someone take care of the horses after he delivers the trunk to the ship.

As soon as he is done giving the groom money and directions, he begins walking with me. I carry a black cloth bag designed and sewn by Tilly as a special gift for my trip. He starts talking immediately. "Elina, I see your tears. Are you sure of your decision?"

"Of course I am Father, but I can't help the tears. I love you and my sisters and brothers, and I'll never see you again."

"I think you're wrong there. Amanda's determined to join you within a year. If she expects me to buy her passage, she at least has to prepare herself. You've done a good job. You have gained much knowledge and grown up a great deal in the last two years. Charles is a fortunate man."

I am no more able to make my tears stop than to sprout wings. I finally squeak out, "I can't talk anymore Father, but I will listen."

He nods and is silent for a few minutes. I think I see tears in his eyes also. When we get to a table he wipes it off as well as the benches, and we sit down. "Tilly says she's packed everything she can think of you might need in your trunk. I wouldn't be surprised if the ships charge for the trunk's transport, but I'll take care of it on this end and inquire for you for the next leg of your journey. I still would have liked to have your passage upgraded to first class, but I understand your decision to stay with the tickets Charles purchased for you. Men are a proud breed, and Charles is no different. I know he wanted to pay for your entire trip. I do have this for you, however," he says as he hands over a pouch. "Put it in your satchel before Mrs. Stromberg and Amanda come with our food. There's no need for Amanda to know I'm giving you some emergency funds."

I mumbled a thank you and put the pouch in my satchel.

"Keep it in a safe place, darling. It's probably more money than Charles makes in a year."

"Father, you shouldn't have."

"Perhaps not, but I wanted to, and I did. Now no more about it. Here comes Mrs. Stromberg and Amanda."

And there they were with brown bags of delicious smelling fish. "Ah, fried cod, I believe, and even chips. Ambrosia for sailors and those sailing," Father says, as he digs into the bags pouring the food onto the newspaper pages that have come with. "Did you get beverages?"

"Of course," Tilly says as she brings out bottles of cider and a cruet of vinegar to sprinkle on the fish. We eat quickly, commenting on the deliciousness of the simple food. All but me, that is, who has a terrible time swallowing. The meal is over quickly, and Father mentions he's almost forgotten to talk about tipping the stewards who will load and unload my trunk. "Watch what others are doing, but I don't believe you can ever offend a working man with a tip. It doesn't need to be extravagant, but it should say thank you."

I nod, wondering how I will handle all of the directions Father has given me. "And remember to go on the deck whenever you're able to. I'm told the air in steerage can be foul. Again, a few coins for the steward might get you onto the deck even when it isn't time for steerage passengers to be there. Don't hesitate to try. And now let's get you to the ship."

Father finds his groom, and the two of them carry the trunk to the gangplank. We women follow slowly behind. By the time we reach the ship, Father is talking with a steward. I watch him as he inconspicuously slips money to the man, who whistles to another steward, and the heavy trunk disappears up the gangplank.

"You'll need to have your traveling papers checked as well as your ticket before you board. We're not allowed to accompany you, so it's time for our good-bye hugs, darling Elina. When you get to Hull, you won't have us with you, so check in right away, and get settled on the Orion. Then you can go back up to the deck to say good-bye to England also."

Teary hugs are exchanged, and I hand my paperwork to the next steward, who checks it carefully, and tells me to be careful on the gangplank. I walk carefully, show my ticket to another steward, who guides me, with a look of surprise, to the steerage compartment, which is bustling with noisy families. I find the cot that matches the number on my ticket and am relieved to see my trunk nearby. I find myself suddenly claustrophobic and ill at ease with the commotion, so head back to the deck, which is also crowded but has the advantage of fresh air.

I spot my family, and wave to them. When the ship eventually pulls away from the docks, I am surprised by a wave of emotion, which makes me doubt myself and my decision to move so far away. I know I love Charles but, even though my father and Tilly have done their best to prepare me for it, I am surprised by my sudden fear. I am thankful Tillly has told me about her own "marriage jitters".

The trip to Hull goes smoothly and is made more enjoyable by meeting a young lady, Bergita Larsson, who is also traveling alone in order to meet her husband Erik, who is working in the iron mines north of Duluth. We talk a great deal and make the transition to the Orion, the steamship that will take us to America. Everything goes well, mostly because Father had arranged (I now realized that meant hired) for the steward he'd first met to look after me and my cumbersome trunk. When I see the traveling arrangements in steerage, where I will spend the next two weeks, I feel great unease, but Bergita takes the crowded state and crude surroundings all in stride, and makes everything better by arranging to move to a bunk close to me.

Bergita is from Malmo and is willing to endure any hardship in order to join her husband of two years, with 18 months of those two years spent apart. She has worked as a domestic servant for a family in Gothenburg, and with both Erik's and her savings has finally been able to buy the long-awaited passage. She has been well prepared for the simple meals and primitive sanitation, but seems fine with everything until it dawns on her that our human waste is being thrown overboard. . "The poor fish," she says. I smile at her, knowing I'm thinking, "poor us."

I eventually adapt to the noises, food, and lack of privacy. We spend as much time as allowed on deck, and when we return to steerage, we sit on my trunk, and talk so much, we become fast friends. Bergita's sunny disposition is contagious, and she easily soothes my fears of marriage and life in a new country. She even knows a smattering of English, so before we depart from the Orion, I know several more English words and phrases.

The ship takes us to Montreal, a city in Canada, which is northwest of Duluth, I think. After two weeks on the water, Bergita and I are thrilled to walk on solid ground. We are surprised to hear many languages spoken—Swedish, Norwegian and Finnish by immigrants, and what I think is French, English as well as Spanish and Italian.

We experience the humiliation of an examination of our bodies for defects, but are both found healthy, and we each enjoy a long, hot shower while we take turns watching each other's satchels, and then suffer a stinging spray of our bodies with a strong smelling disinfectant, which is also used on all of our possessions.

Once we are able to claim my trunk, Bergita boldly asks two male travelers if they would carry it to the train station, which is close by. They agree, and after they accomplish their good deed, I remember Father's directions and tip each of them, much to the surprise of the men and Bergita who says "You must be very rich to throw your money away."

When I explain that my Father is wealthy, Bergita asks, "So why would such a lady like you travel in steerage?"

I answer, "Because it was Charles who paid for my passage, and he is not a rich man—not yet, anyway."

We both chuckle at my answer and get ourselves settled in the train that will take Bergita to Hibbing and me to Duluth. Once again, we chatter like lifelong friends, exchange addresses, and promise to keep in touch in America. It is with a heavy heart that I watch my new friend depart, but when I see a young man run up to her and take her into his arms, I recognize the strong love they share for one another. I can only pray a brief prayer, asking that Charles and I will be blessed with the same kind of love.

11

Arrival in Duluth

"How shall we sing the Lord's praise in a strange land?"

Psalms 137:4

The trip from Hibbing to Duluth is only three hours long. I look out the train windows and am enchanted by the endless virgin forests. I know Father will be impressed by the expanse of lumber possibilities, and then I sadly realize that Father will never see these scenes. For the first time in my life I am completely alone, and am very glad I will soon see Charles. I fuss with my hair and clothing, wanting to look pretty for my husband-to-be. And then the moment comes. The train comes to a stop, and the conductor announces "Duluth—everyone off" first in English and then in my beloved Swedish.

A small crowd is gathered by the train, and I soon spot Charles intently searching the passengers as they come off the train. When he sees me, his eyes light up, and I feel a flutter of excitement course through my body. He reaches me quickly and gently takes me into his arms. "My dear, Elina. You are finally here."

His voice is as beautiful as I remembered. I answer, "Yes, my love. I have finally arrived." And then neither of us knows exactly what to say, so we simply look at each other as we hold hands. He tells me I am beautiful and I tell him he looks bigger and stronger than he did when he left.

Finally, Charles tells me Mrs. G. has loaned him a carriage for a few days, since we'd need it for my trunk and for moving the few things he owns. We walk to a large pile of crates and trunks, and I easily spot mine. "It's very heavy, Charles. You'll need another man to lift it."

He appears puzzled, but as he tests an end, he knows I am correct and asks an attendant if he would assist him after he moves the carriage closer. They agree on a price for his help, and Charles leaves to get the carriage, returning very quickly. The trunk is loaded, and Charles helps me onto the carriage seat. "I have a room for you tonight at the boarding house. Will you need anything from your trunk before we take it to our house?"

"No, Charles. Everything I need is in my bag. I'd love to see our house though."

"Then, let's go there. It's very humble, but there simply isn't suitable housing available at a price I can afford." He leads the horses away from the train station. Between buildings I can peek a large body of water, which I suppose is Lake Superior, but then I become very interested as we move away from what I suspect is the main part of the city and ride past hundreds and hundreds of shacks.

"What is this place, Charles?"

"It's called Shanty Town or Swede Hill where many hundreds of immigrants--mostly Swedes and Finns—live. Mrs. G. told me I couldn't move you into a shanty. She helped me find a place. It's not grand or anything, but it's a little better than a shanty."

I feel relieved and thankful for Mrs. G., and then Charles stops in front of a row of tiny houses. "Well, this is it. Let's have you take a look at it."

In truth, the house is not very impressive. It is made of unpainted wood, and one wall is covered with tar paper. I can see one window and a couple of small sheds in back of the house.

Charles ties up the horse, and then walks up onto a porch. "Come on, Elina—if you want to see it."

I follow him up the rickety porch and watch him unlock the door, revealing the one room that makes up the house. There are rough lumber walls and a floor of rough boards. A sturdy cook stove sits in the middle of the room, a bed in the corner, and a crude table and two chairs in another corner. "I've slept here the past two nights just to make sure the house isn't broken into. It's quieter than the boardinghouse. So what do you think?"

What I am thinking is that the entire house is smaller than the bedroom I had shared with Amanda and that it is very dark and dreary, nothing like the large, bright rooms in which I have lived, and I have no idea why anyone would want to break into it. What I say is, "It will be fun to make it look cozier. Do you think we could paint the inside?"

"I don't see why not—though I doubt we'll stay here long. Could you handle it without paint for a year or two?"

"Of course," I say, trying not to reveal my disappointment. . "Now how are we going to get the trunk inside?"

"I know we can't lift it, but we should be able to slide it to the door. I make my living moving heavy things, so I've figured out a thing or two. I'll be right back. Just look around."

I look at the wood stove and notice a good size stack of wood. I also see what must be Charles' work clothes on the bed and feel myself blush at the intimacy of them. I notice there are pegs around the walls which must be intended for holding clothes. Before I can examine anything else, I hear a few thumps and bumps and Charles asking me to help him get the trunk through the door. I follow his directions of pushing while he both lifts and pulls the trunk but know I'm not much help. Nevertheless, Charles manages to get the trunk inside and slide it into the one empty corner.

"What do you have in there? It's very heavy."

"I have many things for our home as well as my trousseau—and even books for us to read."

"I understand things for our home, which is good, and books to read, but what's a trousseau?"

"It's a wardrobe a bride has made, so she won't have to buy any clothing for a while." As I answer, I think of the fancy clothing the trunk contains and know how foolish it is.

"We will have to buy pots and pans and such, but I left that for you, so you can choose what you want. Actually, I had a chance to make a list of things. Read it tonight, and add to it what you need. I set aside one week's pay to help furnish our home."

I knew I would have to get used to simple things and am surprisingly all right with that. I don't realize Charles has moved close to me until he gently puts his arms around me. "Do you know we have never even kissed and yet tomorrow you will be my wife?"

I start to answer, but Charles' lips find mine, and he kisses me with great tenderness and love. I suspect I surprise both of us by responding to him, holding him as close as possible. I smile at him. "We have now definitely kissed."

"And are you ready to marry me tomorrow?"

I am shocked by the thought of marrying him the very next day but know there is no reason to wait. "Yes," I whisper, hoping by tomorrow it somehow will be true.

12

A Good Friend

"Bid the older women.......to train the young women to love their husbands and children."

Titus 2: 3-4

Charles brought me to the boarding house where he had lived and introduces me to Mrs. Gundersson, who embraces me in a hearty hug. "How wonderful! You've arrived, and you're as pretty as Charles told me. Now I have a room ready for you tonight, but first let me give you something to eat," she prattles on, all with a wonderful cheerfulness.

She brings us bowls of steaming stew, fresh bread and tall glasses of milk along with mugs of hot coffee and vanilla pudding. Then she sits down with us at a little corner table in her large kitchen.

She asks me question after question as we eat. It is obvious she cares deeply for Charles, whom she says she worries about because he works so hard and spends nothing on himself, saving all for the love of his life. In the next breath, she offers to help me shop for household items and our first groceries and tells me she wants us to eat our first meal as husband and wife at a restaurant, and that she will pay for it as a wedding gift. She seems to know all about our wedding plans and house, and I soon realize she's helped with the plans for everything.

The food tastes wonderful, and the love expressed by Mrs. Gundersson is greatly appreciated.

After a good night sleep and a breakfast of hot porridge with cream and a mug of coffee I pack up the few things I'd taken out of my satchel and am ready when Charles pulls up in the wagon. We are both wearing the same clothes we had worn the day before, but, not having any idea of the condition of the clothing in my trunk, I know I have to settle for the traveling clothes I've been wearing. Mrs. Gundersson, on the other hand, arrives at the wagon, wearing a satin dress and a hat and gloves.

"You look like you should be the bride, Mrs. G." I say.

"Oh, I chose to make use of my shiny wrappings, but no one can compete with your glowing face, dear," she replies.

"My two best girls look beautiful," adds Charles as he helps us onto the wagon. "Now we have a wedding to go to!"

And that it is how it happened that Charles and I, from two completely different backgrounds, were married on June 8, 1890 at Bethel Lutheran Church in Duluth, Minnesota. The wedding, a very simple one, was conducted by Pastor Gulbranson. Mrs. Gundersson and the pastor's wife were the witnesses. At the insistence of Mrs. G., we have a formal photo taken at the L. W. Liden studio on Superior Street following the ceremony, and then eat lunch at the boardinghouse. Mrs. G. kisses and hugs us both with congratulations, and gives Charles a card with the name of a restaurant where she has not only made reservations for six o'clock but prepaid for the meal. She instructs Charles to show me around Duluth until then, and says she will stop at our house on Monday to visit me while Charles is working.

PART TWO

515 Nineteenth Avenue West, Duluth, Minnesota, North America, 1890

> "So the LORD God caused a deep sleep to fall upon the man, and while he slept took one of his ribs and closed up the place with flesh; and the rib which the LORD had taken from the man he made into a woman and brought her to the man. Then the man said, 'This at last is bone of my bones and flesh of my flesh; she shall be called woman, because she was taken out of man.'"
>
> Genesis 2:21-23

13

Creating a Home

> *"Not that I complain of want; for I have learned, in whatever state I am, to be content. I know how to be abased, and I know how to abound; in any and all circumstances I have learned the secret of facing plenty, abundance and want. I can do all things in him who strengthens me."*
>
> Philippians 4:11-13

Early Monday morning, after a breakfast of eggs, bacon, potatoes and coffee, and a sweet good-bye kiss, Charles leaves for work, reminding me that Mrs. G. will stop sometime that day to see how I am doing.

Alone for the first time since our wedding, I allow myself the luxury of a few tears as I talk to God about my new life:

> *"Dear God, I love Charles. I truly do, and I want to be a good wife for him. Help me to do so, and help me to be satisfied with this dreary little house, and show me how to make it better for both of us. In Jesus Name, Amen."*

My tears release the tension I am feeling, and my prayer restores my peace. I have learned so much about Charles in the past two days. His body has become very lean and muscled by the hard work he has been doing. He remains kind and appreciative and enjoys hearing my reactions to what we see and experience. What has really surprised me is that Charles' faith is much stronger than mine. He thanks God for everything he has. And though he desperately wants a dairy farm, he's given the timing and the way we will have one over to God. I've learned he prays many times each day—not on his knees necessarily like I do before I go to bed, but while he is walking or sitting, or even being married. I don't believe anything could shake his faith. On the other hand, I question everything. This morning, before breakfast, we had prayed together, holding hands. We had always said grace and prayers at Ljungsjömåla, but when Charles prays, he sounds as if he's talking directly to God. I don't understand the depth of his faith, and maybe I never will. I can only hope I will learn from my husband, and that he will be patient with me. But now it is time to stop puzzling and to put the house in order as best I can.

When we had come home from our wedding day dinner, we found that Mrs. G. had delivered a book shelf, an icebox complete with ice, butter, eggs, bacon and cream and several wooden boxes that I have yet to unpack. I start with the nearest box and find a pot large enough for soup, which is wonderful because the only other pan we have is the cast iron fry pan Charles had purchased. There are also mixing spoons, a large and a small mixing bowl and a sheet pan on which to bake.

The wood stove has a shelf above it, and that's where I decide to store the pans and bowls. They seem to be sparkling clean, so I put them away, leaving an empty, strong wooden box. I began to have ideas of having Charles nail the boxes to the wall but decide I'd better wait to make sure Mrs. G. doesn't expect them back. With that I remember that she will visit me sometime today and know I need to be ready to open the door to welcome her in. The June day is already balmy, so I will not need to make coffee, which is fortunate, because I have no coffee or coffee pot. I do have a pitcher of water in the icebox, so I can at least offer a cold drink to Mrs. G. I look at my bedraggled reflection in a mirror and decide I also need to retrieve some things from my trunk.

First thing, I smooth my hair with a brush from my satchel, repositioning my combs and rinse off my face with water from one of three pails Mrs. G. has had brought to the house. There is no pump in the yard, but Charles has told me he'll bring home water each day.

Back to the wooden boxes: the next one is filled with many more useful items: a ceramic pitcher and bowl. I suppose they are for washing and am convinced I am correct when I find two bars of castile soap included. I put the first box I've unpacked upside down and top it with the pitcher and bowl as well as a bar of soap. I'll need to find a flat rock to set the soap on, but that can come later. Maybe I can put things underneath that I don't want out in the open—whatever that might be.

The next box holds clothing for Charles, maybe from the boarding house, or maybe some Mrs. G. is giving him. Charles has told me that Mrs. G's husband died several years ago and that she doesn't have any children, so I don't exactly know where the clothes have come from. Nevertheless, I hang work pants and shirts on pegs and fold underwear and a sweater, which I temporarily set on the bed.

The more I unpack, the more I realize we need a chest of drawers or another shelf to use for clothing. I'll be able to store many things in my trunk, but I believe day-to-day clothing needs should be more accessible.

While unpacking the final box from Mrs. G. I discover a coffee pot, baking soda, baking powder, sugar, coffee and yeast. As if she knows I'm thinking of her, at that moment Mrs. G. knocks on the door, and when she enters, I am able to hug her warmly and thank her for the many gifts. "You gave us so much, Mr. G. You are ever so generous. Thank you. Thank you."

"Elina, you are welcome. It looks as if you are making wonderful progress. I've brought a snack for you and some soup and bread for supper. It's all in this basket, which you're welcome to keep. It's a good one for shopping."

"Thank you again and again. What a treat to have supper provided! Charles told me he might be late tonight because of a big shipment."

"Ya, that's what happens when you work on the docks. Put the soup in the icebox, and let's taste the cookies in the basket. There's a bottle of lemonade too."

"Wonderful," I say as I follow Mrs. G's directions, putting soup in the icebox, putting out wax-paper wrapped cookies and pouring lemonade in glasses I've unwrapped. "This is delicious."

Mrs. G. helps herself to the lemonade, leaving the cookies for Charles and me. "I won't stay long. I have a temperance meeting at one, but tell me what else you need."

"Mrs. G., why would I tell you what we need? You'd just get it for us, and we'd be indebted to you even more."

"Oh no, child. That's not the way it works. The good Lord has blessed me, and my greatest pleasure is helping others, especially Swedish immigrants. I want to help you and Charles have a good life."

"You're too kind. I'm finding we have what we need. Now I just need to figure out how to store it. Charles has already told me he could use the wood from my trunk to make a cabinet, but I'm not quite ready to part with it. Do you know where I could get more of the crates you brought here? We could stack them to have more shelves."

"I can help you with that. But first I need to tell you I'm proud of you. I half suspected I'd find you in tears when I came here today. Charles is very worried he won't be able to provide you with what you were used to in Sweden. He calls you his lady. But I see you're using the resources you've been given very well. Come outside with me, and I can point you in the right direction for more crates."

Together we walk out the door, and Mrs. G. points to her carriage. "Hop on, and I'll take you to the docks—not where Charles works, but where cargo comes in crates. There's almost always empties free for the taking. We ride for no more than ten minutes to a pile of empty crates. Mrs. G. and I claim a dozen, and then return to the little house. This time Mrs. G. stays on the carriage while I unload the sturdy boxes.

"These are perfect, Mrs. G. Thank you again."

"You are welcome, Elina, and thanks for the good visit. Whenever you're lonesome or need something, come see me. I won't bother you and Charles anymore. After all, you are newlyweds."

I blush but say, "You've never bothered us. Thank you again."

Mrs. G. leaves with a wave, and I carry the crates inside. In minutes I have stacked them, three high, against the wall, and am mightily pleased with them. I laugh when I remember the beautifully finished furniture at Ljungsjömåla. The contrast is great, but what I have is very functional and for that I'm thankful.

Once I have filled six of the crates with kitchen utensils and baking items, I decide to move the remaining six closer to our bed, in which I will put clothing. Charles has so little that it takes only a short time. I unpack my satchel next, adding my brush, comb, and mirror to the top of the shelves. The clothing in the satchel smells very sour, and I realize I'll need to wash clothes soon, but will leave that until the next day as I need to ask Charles where to get water for laundry.

I reward myself with a short rest but feel guilty knowing Charles is hard at work, so I unlock my trunk, open the cover wide, and look lovingly at my Swedish belongings. I chuckle to myself as I view a ridiculously fancy parasol, gloves, and lace-edged handkerchiefs, realizing they belong to a completely different life, a life I've left behind. I do unpack my skirts and shirts and under clothes, socks, and a gardening hat, knowing that they, at least, will be put to good use. I hope I'll never regret leaving my old life and feel strongly I won't as long as I have Charles' love.

When I come upon my Swedish Bible I realize I haven't read my Bible since leaving Sweden. Amanda would be ashamed of me. Shaking my head at that strange thought, I know I need to write back home soon also. But right now I will read my Bible. I turn to Genesis where I've placed markers regarding the first marriage, that of Adam and Eve. I read that God made Eve as a helpmate for Adam and immediately thank God for Charles and ask for opportunities to be his helpmate. My greatest desire is to be a good wife—and eventually a good mother.

Charles comes home shortly after four with a package of fish, but I already have Mrs. G's soup and bread ready for him to eat before he returns to the docks for four more hours of unloading ships. I've been told that's the dock work pattern: working extra hard while there are long spring and summer days and then shutting down or working much shorter days when the days grow dark--and cold. I am shocked at how tired and dirty he is. I knead his shoulders and back with my hands while he eats until he asks me to stop because it is relaxing him so much he won't be able to return to work. I agree to walk back with him when he asks me to, so we can spend a little more time together.

It feels good to be outside with Charles, exchanging the happenings of our day. Charles is pleased with the progress I've made and even more pleased when I tell him I intend to plant a small garden the next day with seeds I'd brought from Sweden.

The walk passes quickly, and soon the docks and ships loom in front of us. Charles introduces me to his boss, who says I'm a fortunate woman to be married to such a hard worker. Charles replies, "I'm the fortunate one," as he says good-bye to me.

As I walk back to our neighborhood I see many people, mostly couples with small children. I say hello and introduce myself to anyone who asks my name, happy to meet the many young families. As soon as I get the house settled, I know I'll spend more time outside and will make even more acquaintances. Suddenly, I hope Amanda will come to America soon. It would be wonderful to have a sister nearby with which to talk. Surely, now that we're married she'll accept Charles.

Having seen how hard the men at the dock work, I anticipate Charles will be hungry again when he arrives home for the night. I put the soup in the warming oven after I've built a fire to heat water for washing myself and the supper dishes.

Eager to find seeds to plant the next day, I explore in my trunk a bit more, finding not only seeds for lettuce, radishes, sunflowers and nasturtiums which should thrive even though it's already June, but a few hand gardening tools also. I put them all in the basket Mrs. G. has left for me and then take out paper and my fountain pen. I write my first letter to my family, so they will know I have made it to America safely:

> 12 June 1890
> My dear family, including Tilly,
>
> I have made it safely to America and am now married to Charles Soderberg. Funny, this is the first time I've realized my name is Elina Soderberg.
>
> Charles started back to work today. The docks are about a mile from our little home. I spent the day unpacking and organizing. I will start cooking tomorrow. Mrs. Gundersson, Charles' old landlord, has been very generous to us, providing many meals and household equipment.
>
> Our house is very humble but adequate. There are so many immigrants that there is not enough housing for everybody.
>
> Duluth is a very new city. Most of the buildings are wooden, and the streets are still more like dirt-packed paths. I don't know much about it yet, but I will tell you more as I learn about it.
>
> Thank you for all of your kindness.
> With love,
> Charles & Elina Soderberg

I would need to ask Charles how and where to mail my letter, so I set it on the table to remind myself to do so. I'll also need to buy a few groceries, so my hard-working husband can have a little variety in his diet.

He arrives home just as it is getting dark, pleased I'd anticipated his hunger and desire to wash. I watch him soap up and rinse his chest, arms and face and ask shyly if I can help him. He appreciates having me wash his back and then sits down to more soup and all of the bread, butter and cookies I have. He drinks glass after glass of milk and then cups of coffee. When I tell him I'd like to buy groceries the next day, he tells me he is keeping his savings under the straw mattress we share. He asks me to keep my spending under three dollars each week, if possible, so we can continue his savings plan. I agree, a little reluctantly, but know he is a wonderful saver or I wouldn't be here. He can barely keep his eyes open long enough to climb into bed and immediately falls asleep beside me as I listen to the soft sleeping sounds he makes and am delighted that I am married to him.

And that is how the summer work weeks go by: Long days of work, six days a week with Charles near exhaustion every night. I plant a little garden, and we enjoy the fresh lettuce, radishes and spinach. I also love picking the nasturtiums to put in a jar on the table. I learn where the post office, general store, and fish house are and learn to make my three dollars a week for groceries last, as long as we eat mostly fish, eggs and potatoes. I begin baking bread and biscuits to get another saving, and after asking for help in finding fruit to pick, add wild strawberries, raspberries and fresh blueberries before the summer is over. I dry some of the fruit and make jam from what we don't eat fresh. I learn where to get free water for laundry and where to buy pure water for drinking. My days are sometimes long, but I meet a few people in the neighborhood who I quickly call friends and begin knitting and reading in my free time.

My life is very different, but I am in no way disappointed. Love makes all the difference, and Charles is very easy to love.

14

The Blessing of Sundays

"O sing to the LORD a new song; sing to the LORD, all the earth! Sing to the LORD, bless his name; tell of his salvation from day to day. Declare his glory among the nations, his marvelous works among all the peoples!"

Psalms 96: 1-3

We both wait impatiently for each Sunday, the one day we have together, and we cherish each and every moment. I've become very clever, even having meals in the icebox already prepared so I don't have to waste our together time. We usually sleep late, have a lazy breakfast and then walk to the Bethel Lutheran Church. We often take a picnic lunch with us and set out hiking after the church service and coffee following it. I've met many Swedes, who already know Charles and seem delighted that he now has a wife. I've had a chance to hold many new babies and am beginning to wonder when our first baby will be born.

We love to hike either down to Lake Superior to sit on the rocks and have our simple lunch or, when we feel more ambitious, we hike "up the hill" where we have glorious views of Lake Superior and Duluth. Even since my arrival in June, I can notice new buildings popping up in the city.

Charles surprises me when he says he would like to purchase a cow. I know that during the summer months I'll be the one to take care of it. One day he comes home early because of a thunderstorm and asks me if it is a good time to choose a cow.

We laugh as we run through the rain about half a mile farther up the hill from our house where we find a young cow that Charles has already arranged to buy from a man with whom he works. The owner, Alfred Jensen, gives us a rope, milking stool, and pail, along with the cow for the ten dollars Charles gives him. "She's a beauty," the men agree, but then Charles winks at me, letting me know he thinks I am the true beauty.

The rain stops, so we start out for home, only to be drenched again by the time we get the cow situated in the shed in our backyard. After bringing her water and handfuls of grass, we strip off our wet clothes, spreading them over our table to dry, while we rejoice over our cow and each other. Now, if the good Lord blesses us with children, our life will be perfect.

15

The Blessings of Family

*"Look, children are a gift of the Lord,
and the fruit of the womb is a reward."*

Psalm 127:3

In August of 1891, Esther was born. She was delivered by a midwife, who told me my wide hips gave me a body *made* to have children. Charles and I rejoice as our little girl thrives. We expect she will be the first of a large, healthy family.

Charles continues to put in long, hard hours at the docks with the motivation of purchasing a farm as soon as possible. He confides in me that he knows he won't be able to work at the docks forever, thinking he will try to do it for ten years, but is afraid his back will give out before then.

My life revolves around Charles and Esther. I do everything I can to be a good wife and mother. I have become just as frugal as Charles, finding ways to stretch the three dollars I allow myself to spend on groceries weekly. With the addition of our cow I am now able to make our butter and cheese. The young cow is already yielding close to three gallons of milk each day, and I use our surplus to barter with appreciative neighbors for just about anything they have. We've also added a few hens to our family, so we no longer need to buy eggs.

I have also become very resourceful in finding items for the house. I walk daily and regularly check items marked "free", and have been able to claim rugs, old clothing which I make into clothing for Esther, and my favorite find, used books. I am amazed that people would discard such wonderful items. I've put curtains made from flower sacks over our open shelves, and they look cozy. Close to the time of Esther's birth, while I was walking, a lady offered me a buggy, which I gladly accepted. Now I can continue my walks with Esther, who is an easy baby for which to care. I take her on a buggy ride daily, believing the fresh air and sunshine is good for both of us. Occasionally, I walk to the docks to watch the men work. When I spot Charles I'm always shocked at his heavy loads, and I continuously pray for his safety.

Once a week I bring Esther to Mrs. G's boardinghouse, so she can admire our little girl. Without children of her own, Mrs. G. has taken the role of a doting grandmother and frequently lavishes clothing or a simple toy on Esther as well as "finding" food items she "has no use for" to give to me. Charles does not have time to visit her, but Mrs. G. always asks about her "favorite young man."

Summer turns to fall, and I am thrilled to have Charles' hours at the dock cut once again. He is fascinated by our little girl, enjoying holding her and reading to her out of the Bible and newspaper. Esther is perfectly content, unless she is hungry or wet, and she continually follows us with her eyes, which isn't very hard to do in a one room house.

When cold weather arrives, a family of mice move into the house. Charles solves that problem with the adoption of a kitten, enjoyed by both Esther and me.

It has been an especially harsh winter with lots of snow, including blizzards now and then. I've hated feeling the wind blow between the boards in our walls, and I wrap Esther in many layers to keep her warm. I've also stuffed rags between gaps in the walls, especially where the wall meets the floor, and Charles and I have piled snow up against the outside walls of our little house. Though it makes no sense to me, he tells me the snow insulates the house from cold. Whether it makes sense or not, the drafts have subsided. Charles told me there were advantages to being raised in poverty since he had learned many tricks for survival.

16

Costly Love

"In a moment they will die, and the people will be troubled at midnight and pass away, and the mighty will be taken away without a hand."

Job 34:20

In the spring of 1892, I receive word that Amanda is coming to Duluth. I excitedly await her arrival and write to her that she is welcome to stay in our humble abode until she decides where she wants to live.

Esther and I meet her at the train in May. She comes off the train looking exactly like the elegant lady she is. I look down at my faded skirt as she walks towards us in an elegant dress, hat and gloves. We hug, and she admires Esther, who is happily sitting in her buggy.

"Isn't she too old to be in a buggy?" Amanda asks.

"Perhaps, but it works well for walking with her," I reply.

We arrive at our little house after hiring a wagon to take us and Amanda's trunk. I have spent many days scrubbing and polishing to make everything look as good as it can. I've baked breads and sweets I believe Amanda will enjoy, and I've placed a bouquet of lilies of the valley on the table and feel pleased with my work. As soon as I open the door, I can feel my sister's disproval. "This is where you've been living?" she asks in disbelief.

"Yes, Amanda. I told you there's little housing for immigrants. Building hasn't kept up with the demand. I know it's temporary, and it keeps us warm and dry."

"Where would I sleep?" she asks.

"You'll have Esther's bed, and she'll sleep with Charles and me."

"I don't think so, Elina. I'm glad we didn't have the driver unload my trunk. I'll check out the boarding houses instead. I certainly don't want to be an inconvenience to you."

I am disappointed. I'd been looking forward to having a sister nearby, and somehow I thought she'd be able to accept my living conditions, but I was sorely wrong.

Esther and I walk her to the hired buggy. Esther jabbers on, but Amanda and I are silent. I wonder when, or if, I'll see her again.

In 1894 Rosa arrives, but she does not seem to have the strength to nurse and remains small and frail until she dies at three months of age. Charles and I are crushed by the loss. Our pastor assures us that God knows our sadness and will give us more children.

Hulda, a healthy, strong baby is born in March of 1895. By then Esther is four and loves to "help" care for Hulda. We continue "buggy walks", as Esther calls them, with Hulda in the buggy and Esther walking along. Strangers often stop to see the baby and to talk to Esther, who is outgoing and entertaining. We often come home with Esther clutching a stick of candy or even a coin given to her by her "new friend."

Before Hulda is even walking, I realize I am again pregnant and pray the child will be a boy. Just as Hulda's walking becomes more confident, Anna arrives on June 14th, 1896. She appears healthy, but one morning when she is five months old, I find her dead in her cradle. Once again, I am heartbroken and seem unable to care for the family. I start doing chores and stop in the middle to sit down to cry, leaving Charles to care for Esther and Hulda. I can tell he is worried, and he finally confronts me. "Elina, we have lost two beautiful girls, and we can't do anything about it. Now Esther and Hulda need your care, and I must return to the docks."

I look at him with tear-filled eyes and say, "I simply don't know what I've done to make God so angry."

"Our babies didn't die because of anything you did. Death and sickness came with the fall of man, but God will pull us through it."

"What does he know about death or how I feel?"

"Elina, try to understand. Every time we love someone we put ourselves at risk for hurt and loss. Love is costly. Think of what you gave up when you fell in love with me. You left your position as a manor lady to live in a one-room, poorly built shack."

"That's different, Charles." I chose to give up my position and would do so again many times over."

"I'm glad to hear that Elina, but, by nature people disappoint one another by their words and actions. Sometimes they try to be hurtful, and sometimes it just happens. Think of how hurt you were when Amanda rejected our house. You, no doubt, were just as shocked the first time you saw it, but chose to accept it. Children can be disrespectful or not as perfect as we want. One of us will die and leave the other brokenhearted. Esther and Hulda will die sometime, hopefully long after we're gone, but simply knowing they too will die is painful.

"As to what God knows about loss and death, just think, Elina. He created a beautiful world and mankind to occupy it, but the first people He made, Adam and Eve, chose not to obey the one rule He made, not to eat the apple. Then their first son murdered his own brother, and people have lived sinfully ever since. But did God give up? No, instead He sacrificed His son—His only son, Jesus, who was perfect. And He did it for us, for sinners. How can you possibly say He knows nothing of how you feel?"

"Charles, your faith is strong, much stronger than mine."

"Perhaps. Before you came to me, God was the only one I could count on, and I learned to depend upon him at an early age, but that's beside the point. It's time for you to make peace with God, so He can comfort you. It won't happen all at once. I'm not foolish enough to believe that you'll suddenly stop grieving, but let Him be with you. I know you're busy with the little girls, but take time to read the Bible and pray. It's the only way you'll be able to weather this storm—or any other."

"I will try, Charles. I will try." We hold each other for a long time, both grieving in our own way. Life was very difficult for me for a long time, but never as difficult as that evening when Charles shared his spiritual wisdom with me. It opened up a closeness and communication I expect we'll share for the rest of our lives. Though I struggled with my grief for a long time, I always returned to Charles' words which were a source of comfort and eventually strength.

It is so easy to realize that many babies die, that in their first year of life, they are extremely vulnerable. As I talk with women, few have been spared the loss of a child through miscarriage, stillbirth, or death. Maybe a hundred years from now, that will change, but now survival of an infant is not a sure thing. I know that. I do. But it's so different when it's the child that has been growing in my womb that dies. Anna and Rosa were part of me, and now they're gone.

Much to my surprise, Amanda has become a help to me. She gave up on her plan to become a teacher and after six months as a domestic servant married August Hall, a successful lumberjack. They have built a fine house and live about ten miles from us in a community of Swedes called Adolph. I had lost track of where she even lived, but we coincidentally made use of the same midwife, who told Amanda I had lost two little girls. Amanda has begun to visit me while Charles is at work, saying she never wants to be with my husband because he "dragged me into poverty." Though I'm saddened by her attitude, I overlook it because I treasure our growing closeness. She has also lost a baby, and we spend hours off and on talking about our pain. It prevents me from needing to share those feelings as often with Charles. I have become convinced that men cannot totally understand a woman's loss of a child, no matter how hard they try.

17

From Sweetness to Sorrow

"The snares of death encompassed me; the pangs of Sheol laid hold on me; I suffered distress and anguish. Then I called on the name of the LORD."

Psalms 116:3, 4

It is 1897, and life is sweet for Charles and me. Esther is a bright five-year-old, who will start school in the fall. Hulda, a surprisingly quiet toddler, follows her big sister everywhere.

We have learned that there are small farms to rent in West Duluth, and we are trying to decide if that's what we should do or stay where we are, waiting to move until we have saved enough money for a down payment on land. We pray for guidance, and both feel we are being told to wait as there has been no clear answer.

One morning Charles goes to work as usual, kissing us all good-bye, telling his daughters to be good, and that he'll be back for supper.

It is a washday for me, and as soon as Charles leaves I heat water, adding slivers of lye soap. I had found a washboard in a giveaway heap earlier in the year, and I start my pile of laundry as Esther patiently "reads" to her little sister, keeping her far away from the dangerous hot water. I move from bed sheets to underwear and then to diapers, which have been soaking. I wring out each of the garments with my reddened hands and then hang them outside on our clothesline. When I go outside to move our cow to a new grazing area, I am surprised to hear Alfred, the man who sold us his cow, call my name. I look over to the road, which runs behind our house and see Charles lying in a wagon.

Why was Charles home so early I think to myself, but as I move closer to the wagon, I see he has been badly injured. Blood-soaked bandages are wrapped around his head, and his eyes are black and blue and swollen almost shut. It looks as if he's been in a violent fight, but that doesn't make any sense.

Alfred Jensen helps him, as he says, "It looks worse than it is, Mrs. Soderberg. At least that's what the doctor said when he sewed him up. Let's get him inside, and I'll tell you more."

With one arm around Alfred and one around me Charles is slowly able to make it inside and onto our mattress on which I toss a fresh sheet.

Alfred continues "He was hit by a barrel that fell when the sling carrying it above him, broke. It got him right on his noggin—peeled his skin right off his forehead. The doc sewed him up and said he needs to rest till the swelling goes down. He took a vial of liquid from his pocket and said "use a few drops of this laudanum in water to help with pain, and put ice on his forehead. The bandage needs to be changed in the morning, but don't touch the stitches. I'll check back tonight, and the doc will stop tomorrow."

"You look awfully pale, Mrs. Soderberg. Are you all right?"

"Ya, sure, I'm okay," I respond as I feel my entire body begin to shake.

"Well, I'll see you tonight then. Oh, don't let him move around either. Good-bye."

"Thank you. I'll see you tonight and the doctor tomorrow."

Alfred leaves. I close the door tightly, locking it also, something I hardly ever do. I have a need to lock out any other bad news from our house, but bad news has already arrived. I pull my chair to the bed and hold Charles' hand. His eyes remain closed, but at my touch he says, "I'm sorry. I saw it falling, but I couldn't move fast enough."

"It looks bad, Charles. How does it feel?"

"Just like it must look. The doc gave me some medicine. I'll need more in an hour or so."

Esther and Hulda climb ono the bed, looking carefully at their father. Esther asks very seriously, "Why does Father have a nappy around his head?"

"They're bandages, Esther. He hurt himself. I'd like you and Hulda to stay off the bed now. We don't want to bump him. It might hurt."

They obediently clamber off the bed and go back to their books. I pray Charles will heal and then don't know what to do next.

After simply gazing at his horribly injured head for way too long, I know I have to prepare for whatever will happen next. I begin working automatically, one step at a time, trying hard not to look at my husband, whose mere sight instantly brings on tears. How could this terrible event have happened?

First, I empty the large pot of water I'd used for washing clothes. Esther says she's hungry, so I heat up last night's supper and give her soup and bread. It is past Hulda's lunch also, so I quickly change her nappy and feed her while she sits in her highchair. When she is contented, I put her in her little bed and take some soup for myself. While cleaning up, I hear Charles mumbling and go to him, asking if he needs medicine. When he says he does, I give him the medicine and ask if he wants something to eat. "No, not now, Elina. I just need to sleep. His eyes, what I can see of them, are bright red and filled with pain, but there seems to be nothing more I can do for him but pray and continue my meaningless tasks.

I have fish in the icebox that need to be cooked, whether or not anyone wants to eat them so that is my next job, followed by starting bread for the next day and moving the cow to a new grazing area, which I was about to do when I'd first seen Charles arrive.

Before I go outside, I ask Esther to watch both Charles and Hulda in case they need anything, and Esther takes the responsibility very seriously. After moving the cow, I check the clothes and find they are dry, so gather them and bring them into the house. That gives me the job of folding the clothing and ironing the shirts, skirts and dresses. To heat the iron, I rebuild the fire which I have carelessly allowed to die down to nothing. I use the table on which to iron and find solace in the steady slap, slap, slap of the iron against the wrinkled clothing. I fold the laundry, placing garments with extra care neatly on a shelf.

Soon after I've finished the ironing, Alfred stops by, bringing us pails of water, which he adds to the barrel that stands outside the house door. He also gathers an armful of wood to take inside with him and then sits by Charles and visits for a few minutes. He pulls an envelope from his pocket and hands it to Charles, telling him the fellows wanted him to have the money inside to tie him over till he can work again.

"Look at this, Elina. The fellows took up a collection for us. Put it in a safe place."

With his errands done, Alfred reminds us that the doctor will check tomorrow. I thank him for his help and for the collection and say good-bye.

Always the money manager, Charles asks me to count the money, and I find ten dollars and a few cents in the envelope.

"That will keep us in groceries for a few weeks, but we'll have to dip into our savings for our next rent," I say, as if Charles doesn't have enough to worry about.

"Ya, and we'll need a couple dollars for the doctor tomorrow too. The good Lord has provided once again."

I wanted to tell him it was his friends who had given him the money and "the Good Lord" hadn't honored my prayer of safety for my husband, but Charles has actually perked up a bit, and I say nothing to interfere with his renewed spirits.

I feed him supper while he leans on pillows on the bed. He actually seems to enjoy the fish and potatoes and the lettuce and beans from our garden. He is very thirsty and drinks glass after glass of water. He relieves himself in a jar, which I empty in the outhouse before milking the cow and putting it inside for the night. I had planned to make butter that day, but Charles' accident had interfered, so now I have an icebox full of milk and more to add to it. I fill all of the bottles I have, putting the cream in the butter churn, wondering if I could pay the doctor tomorrow with butter or milk.

The morning comes quietly after what seems to have been close to a sleepless night. Charles, as is his routine, needs to use the outhouse, so I help him outside only to hear the cow bawling to be milked. I get Charles back inside and help him to lie down. He is shivering greatly this morning, something I've never seen him do before, so I cover him with blankets and hurry outside to milk Bessie, after washing her udder. Once Bessie is milked, given water and mash, I move her to the backyard where she can graze contentedly.

Back in the house, I refuel the fire and put on coffee and oatmeal. Hulda is already awake, so I change her nappy and put her dress, stockings and shoes on. She sits in her highchair, waiting for her oatmeal, while Esther who has wakened plays peek-a-boo with her.

After giving Esther her breakfast I help Charles to oatmeal and coffee. Because of the mess he is making, I would like to feed him also, but I know he wants to do what he can on his own. I clean up Hulda and Charles, and then remind him I'm to change the bandages today.

"You might as well get at it then before I fall asleep." I unwind the bandages which are saturated with blood. Once they are off I am frightened by what I see: Just as I'd been told, his entire forehead has been peeled off and is now reattached by angry, black stitches. I count over a hundred before Charles asks me what I'm looking at.

"You've been stitched back up by a careful doctor, but you're still bleeding a bit. Alfred left gauze pads and more bandaging, so I'm going to put them on now." I carefully lay the gauze over the area that is bleeding and then wrap the bandages around his head. I sense him wince a few times, so know he is still hurting badly. When I offer him more laudanum, he accepts it gratefully. "Elina, thank you for helping. I'm sorry to give you another job to do, but I'd like you to count the money we've saved. We're going to have to do some planning."

I don't see what plans are open for us except to wait until Charles heals, so he can go back to work. Nevertheless, I count the savings of a little over forty dollars—enough for two months' rent plus money for food. I know Charles will hate to spend our savings, but what else can we do?

I tell Charles my counting results, and he says simply, "That's not nearly enough."

I assume he is thinking of our plans to put a down payment on land and say, "Remember we still have the money Father gave us."

"That's yours, dear Elina. We've talked about it before. When we have our own house built, I want you to use that money for furniture and any other extras you desire."

I know better than to say anything but can see where that money could be easily used up to pay our current rent and keep us fed. I have no idea how long it will take Charles to heal. I can only hope the doctor will give us good news when he stops tonight.

18

God Provides

"And we know that all things work together for good to them that love God, to them who are the called according to his purpose."

Romans 8:29

It is close to sunset when we hear someone knocking on the door. When I open it, with Esther and Hulda holding onto my skirt, I see two strange men, who immediately introduce themselves as Harry Gundersson, Charles' boss and brother-in-law of Mrs. G., and Dr. Monson, who I'm told repaired Charles' head. I lead them into the house to Charles' bed, where he lies awake, and I light another kerosene lamp to help the doctor examine Charles.

"Well, Charles, it looks as if you have a good nurse. Your bandages have been changed and are spotless," says Dr. Monson. "Can you sit up for me?"

Mr. Gundersson helps him sit up while I put pillows behind his back. Without another word the doctor unwinds the bandages and examines

Charles' head. He presses against his forehead in a few places and then announces, "You're healing is progressing well, but it's going to take a long time before you feel normal." He holds the kerosene lamp closer to Charles' eyes and says, "Not only have you torn off a great deal of skin, but you've had a concussion. You're truly fortunate to be alive. I don't see any reason for you not to return to normal though you might have recurring headaches, and you might suffer from dizziness." With that said he paints Charles' forehead with some kind of orange medicine, and when it dries, rewraps his head with fresh bandages.

"I'll leave more bandages and more laudanum. You should change his dressings daily, Mrs. Soderberg, and if you keep them as clean as they were today, there should be no infection. If it smells foul, however, come see me. I'll leave my card so you can find me."

"Thank you, Dr. Monson. How much do I owe you?"

"Nothing, Mrs. Soderberg. I've taken care of it," says Charles' boss. "Thanks, Monson. How about we make another trip here in about a week?"

"Sounds good to me, Harry. Now if there are no more questions, I'll be on my way to my next house visit," he continues as he leaves our house.

"So these are your two little girls, Charles. You've described them and their hard-working mother well. Don't try to hurry back to work. Next time I come we'll talk about a little different position for you."

Neither Charles nor I know what he means by a different position, but we are encouraged, nevertheless.

"You'll be all right. God is good."

"We know He is, Mr. Gundersson. And thank you for your help too," I say as I show him to the door.

The next week goes by slowly. I have my hands full caring for Charles and our two little girls. Actually, Esther is a big help, and I'm not sure how I would have done everything without her. I know Esther will start school in two months and can only hope that by then Charles will be well. I haven't told him yet, but I feel certain I am once again pregnant.

The doctor makes another visit, removes the stitches and reassures us that everything is progressing well, and that the bandages are no longer needed. He encourages Charles to move around as much as he can but not to lift anything heavier than a few pounds, and by all means not to return to the docks. Before he leaves, he tells us Gundersson was unable to make it that evening, but plans to see us soon.

The next day it rains hard from early morning on. Charles remarks that no one would be working on the docks today. Esther is happy cutting out paper dolls and clothing while Hulda watches and plays with the left over scraps of paper and cardboard. Charles tries to read his Bible, but one of his frequent headaches interferes, and he finally pulls his chair over to the table to play quietly with his little girls.

A knock on the door surprises us all, and Mr. Gundersson enters with Mrs. G, who hugs me and scolds me for not getting word to her that Charles had been in an accident. "Here, I had to wait for my brother-in-law to tell me your news. If I'd known, I would have come sooner. She then coos over the girls, handing them each a storybook before examining Charles' head and telling him he looks terrible. Those words surprise me, but I suppose I've gotten used to seeing the raw skin that still sags over his eyes.

"Now my brother-in-law has much to say to you, so I'm going to play paper dolls with my friends Esther and Hulda, and then we'll empty my basket to put lunch on the table." As always, no one can resist her enthusiasm and friendly nature.

Mr. Gundersson sits down on our trunk and asks us to pull up chairs, which we do. He has a notebook in his hands, on which he's written many numbers, all of which are mysteries to us.

"I'm not going to take credit for this plan. It was Mary who straightened me out letting me know what a terrible employer I've been." He smiles as he talks, letting us feel Mary has the upper hand—once again, but that he is enjoying following her advice.

"Anyway, my friend, Doc Monson has told me you're not to work at the docks any more. He says he doesn't know how long you might have headaches and dizziness. That would make you a danger to yourself and to everyone else on the docks. To tell you the truth, I'm surprised you're alive and doing as well as you are. When I saw the barrel hit you, I was one of many who thought you were dead."

"So what are we to do?" I ask with tears running down my cheeks. "Without a job, we'll use up our savings quickly, and then be destitute."

Charles reaches for my hand, whispering for me to just listen.

"Thanks, Charles, that's what I want both of you to do. Mary's told me you've been saving money for a farm—planning to rent first and then buy one to raise dairy cows. You both seem well-fitted for that vocation, and I know you've been working hard so your dreams will come true. Mary checked on the cost of renting a place in West Duluth and found you can get a decent plot of land for grazing, a barn that could hold ten cows and a small house for forty dollars a month. It helps that it's my land, and I've had the renters give me notice since they've put down money on a place they're planning to buy.

"Anyway, you can move in rent-free for the coming year. It's too late, of course, to plant anything this year, so I have some money in this envelope which I'll call back pay to help you with groceries and hay for the next year. Oh, yes, and enough to buy nine cows. That should give you a good start, and in a year, I expect to start getting my rent."

"Mr. Gundersson, that is so kind of you. I didn't know what I was going to do," mumbles Charles through tears. "Words are not adequate to thank you."

"You can thank Mary and me by having more children, and name your next girl, Mary, and your first son Harry."

"Of course, we'll do that," I say, and you can come for milk or cream anytime you want."

"Let's shake on that," Harry Gundersson says, and then we sit at the table to enjoy Mrs. G's stew, bread, and rice pudding. She looks very smug as she dishes up food and tells us her driver and wagon will arrive a week from today to move us to West Duluth. "I filled Harry's wagon with empty crates for you to pack up once they dry out."

"You can see Mary was very confident you'd agree to our plan," Mr. Gundersson adds with a chuckle.

"How could we resist?" I ask, with the first smile on my face since Charles has been injured.

PART THREE

Life on 46ᵗʰ Avenue West

"…and to bring them up out of that land to a good and broad land, a land flowing with milk and honey."

Exodus 3:8

19

The First Soderberg Farm

"And God said, 'Let the earth bring forth living creatures according to their kinds: cattle and creeping things and beasts of the land according to their kind...'"

Genesis 1: 24

The next few weeks are a whirlwind of activity. I take the buggy and Hulda to our landlord, telling him we will be leaving. Having heard of Charles' accident, he shows surprising mercy by not even asking us to pay any more rent though we will be spending a few days of September in our little house

Charles and I go to the neighboring houses telling our friends we are leaving and thanking them for their help while Charles was in such bad shape. They had brought us water and firewood and even some food. Charles couldn't walk the distance up the hill to Alfred Jensen's house, so I did so by myself, asking him to thank the dock workers for their collection and to tell them where we'd be moving. I also walk to church on

Sunday, again alone, to thank Pastor Anderson and to tell him we were leaving. He had not heard of Charles' injury, and offers prayer and his encouragement for healing. He also has a few Bible story picture books he asks me to give to Esther to entertain herself and little Hulda.

Mrs. G's driver, Sven, arrives on the third of September, just as promised, and he and I load the wagon with crate upon crate and tie the cow to the back. He says he'll be back for the trunk, the icebox, the table, chairs, and beds after he's unloaded everything. At the last minute, he asks if Charles would like to go with the first load, and Charles says yes, and that he'd like to take Hulda with also. Charles has taken over much of Hulda's care while he's been recuperating, and I appreciate his generous offer, leaving Esther and me to finish the last bit of packing and cleaning.

When Sven returns, a couple of hours later, I am done, but Esther is beside herself because she can't find her cat, "Kitty," and has no intention of leaving until it appears. Sven has enlisted the assistance of another man, and together they load the furniture, including the heavy trunk. By then, Esther has found Kitty and holds her tightly in her arms. Sven helps Esther and Kitty get settled in the back of the wagon, while I, feeling completely exhausted, climb up next to Sven. On we go to the new farm that I have not even seen. I can only hope that it meets Charles' approval and that he is feeling pleased at the moment. I say a silent prayer, asking God to give peace and gratitude to Charles and to me.

The few miles go by quickly, even in the heavy-laden wagon, and I am surprised as rows of houses give way to small farms. Though we are not far from our old house, I feel as if this area is a hidden treasure that we are about to discover. There is still the steep hill west of us and the Lake, though not visible, must be east of us, but I've not seen this neighborhood before. Suddenly, Sven interrupts my thoughts, saying, "Well, here you are Mrs. Soderberg. You've got a pretty place here."

He pulls up to a house, far larger than the one we've left, but still simple in design. Charles comes out of the house with Hulda in his arms. "Elina, it's a beautiful spot. Look at the good pasture, and the barn is bigger than I imagined. The water from the well is wonderful, also."

Sven and his helper unload the trailer, asking me where I want everything. I start with a similar arrangement as in our last house, but am thrilled to see there are two rooms, one of which will be used as a bedroom. Someone has thoroughly swept the house, and when I find a familiar basket filled with sandwiches, apples, cookies and lemonade, I recognize Mrs. G's touch. What a great friend she is!

Sven leaves, and I notice how fatigued Charles looks. I put the sandwiches, fruit and lemonade on the table and put Hulda in her highchair. With everyone's stomach filled, the cow happily grazing, and Kitty purring in Esther's arms, I make up the bed for Charles who decides he needs another dose of laudanum to ease the pounding in his head. That done, I change Hulda's nappies and put her in bed with Charles who is already gently snoring.

Esther and I explore inside and out. I am thrilled to find a water pump in the kitchen, which is a wonderful convenience. I taste the water, finding it sweet and cold, which is also a blessing.

Esther runs with joyous abandon, looking at everything, announcing that even the outhouse smells good. When I check on Hulda, finding her fast asleep, I tell Esther that I need to rest awhile before starting to unpack. I tell Esther she can stay outside as long as she can see the house where ever she goes. Esther easily agrees to those boundaries, and I fall fast asleep as soon as I lay down on the unmade trundle bed.

20

New Beginnings

"Thou wilt keep him in perfect peace, whose mind is stayed on thee: because he trusteth in thee."

Isaiah 26:3

During the next few days, the four of us settle into our new home. I unpack the crates and continue to make shelves out of the empties. Charles is delighted with the barn, and he spends time in it, planning where he will erect stalls and an area for our chickens. He cannot remain upright for any length of time, but his mood continues to be very positive. He often sits with paper and pencil listing things he'll need for the farm and how he expects to pay for it. When he is inside and not making lists, he spends most of his time with Esther and Hulda, continuing to be an excellent, attentive father.

I take Esther to the Oneota School, which is less than a mile from the farm, and register her for first grade. The school will start the following Tuesday, and Esther is very excited. When I walk Esther to school the first day, little Hulda is absolutely devastated not to be able to follow her big sister into the tall, brick and brownstone school. She sobs all of the way home, but then Charles takes her with him and somehow wears her out so much she falls asleep during lunch, and doesn't wake up until Esther is home with much to tell about her first day as a student.

I am experiencing morning sickness, something I had not experienced in my earlier pregnancies. I secretly hope that symptom means I am carrying a boy. Before the baby arrives, I know I need to help Charles get a good start with our dairy farm. He has located sturdy dairy stock just a mile away from our farm, and he and Esther walk them right down Grand Avenue, in two groups, to our farm, on the Saturday after she began school. I take Hulda in the buggy, even if she is too old at two to fit, and I walk alongside the street for the first trip, watching for traffic, and the trip goes surprisingly well. Hulda and I stay with the first group of cows in their new home, a pen Charles and I had erected for them, as we wait for Charles and Esther to come with the second group.

Following the instructions of my father, I start an account book for the new farm, starting with Saturday, September 10, 1897, the very day we purchased the cows. When I show the book to Charles, he is pleased but tells me I should start at the beginning of the month, entering the expenses of fencing, hay, and miscellaneous tools, including the cream separator, we'd purchased. I agree and carefully erase my entries, so I can keep everything in the correct timeline. That evening we talk about the needs we have and make a plan for what we need to earn in order to keep saving for our own farm, pay our rent starting next September, and keeping up with household expenses. Charles says he needs a horse and wagon, so he can sell our milk, but doesn't want to reduce the gift from Gundersson further. I remind him of the money my father has given us, which we'd put aside to furnish the house we plan to build. As we talk, Charles realizes that buying a horse and buggy is necessary in order to earn the money we need. He says we will use "my gift money" but will definitely pay it back. He reluctantly agrees to begin looking for a horse and buggy, and then asks me to pray with him, regularly seeking God's guidance for our life, including our expenses, and how we run our farm.

One day Charles tells me he's been thinking how good God has been to us, allowing him to have the accident on the dock. "How in the world can you think your accident shows God was good to you? You were almost killed," I needlessly remind him.

"My Elina, just think about it. Almost killed means I'm still alive, and if I hadn't been hurt, we wouldn't have this start to a farm. God used what we thought was a tragedy to bring us here."

I start to shake my head, but as I see the happiness in Charles' eyes, I say, "Someday, Charles, I hope I become wise enough to see things as you do."

"If you ask for wisdom, you'll receive it, dear woman. But don't change too much. I love you just as you are."

I smile at my good husband. "I am ever so thankful God brought you to me."

21

The Routine on a Dairy Farm

"This is the day which the LORD hath made; we will rejoice and be glad in it."

Psalm 118:24

The fall of 1897 is a time of learning for everyone. Esther is a very successful first grader, who is thrilled to be learning to read and write. She thinks everything about school is wonderful and loves to play school with two-year-old Hulda, who is a willing student, though a disappointment to her big sister. Charles and I work well together. Our ten cows thrive, and all but one yields gallons of milk each day. We add twenty chickens to have a good supply of eggs also. While we work on the farm, Charles teaches me English, which I feel is a necessity now that Hulda has begun school.

We start our day, while it is still dark by washing udders and milking the cows. When I have my first pail full of milk, I take it to the house, where I stay, while Charles finishes milking.

If the girls are awake I make breakfast for them. Otherwise, I continue with the milk, separating out the cream and filling our many bottles which I put in our second icebox, which we'd purchased solely for milk. When Charles comes in with the rest of the milk, I wake the girls and/or dress and feed Hulda. With the girls settled, I return to milk duties until all of it is in the icebox. I wash Hulda's hands and face and set her down to play and then eat my own breakfast with Charles. Afterwards, he hitches our horse to the buggy, which he loads with milk in partitioned crates he has built for that purpose. He makes his first deliveries, then returns to pick up Esther to bring her to school and continues on his route. He has had some regular customers, almost from his first day of deliveries, but stops at several other houses to see if the occupants need to buy milk. He returns home by ten in the morning, sometimes with leftover milk, which we date and return to the icebox, and sometimes he comes home with all of the milk sold.

On normal days, by the time he returns home, I am busy cleaning bottles, or making cheese or butter. On Mondays, however, I wash our clothes and hang them outside to dry. I also make beds, tidy the house, and start any cooking that needs to be done for the day. Charles feeds and brings water to the chickens, mucks out the barn, adds new hay, as needed, puts in feed and water for the cows, and completes additional chores such as removing rocks and preparing gardening spaces for the following spring, if he has sufficient energy.

During the first winter on our little farm, Charles and I spend much time planning improvements. We will have a garden, growing carrots, potatoes, rutabagas, beets, lettuce, spinach, beans and tomatoes in enough quantity to keep us supplied with vegetables during the winter. I am pleased to find rhubarb growing on the farm land and feel confident I'll find wild raspberries, strawberries, and blueberries in the hills behind us. We both decide not to overdo the gardening since we are very aware of the baby due in March. The next year we plan to enlarge gardens enough to be able to sell produce along with the dairy products. Charles says he would like to add even more chickens to have more eggs for sale since more of his milk customers are asking for them. As

Charles says, "That is the beauty of farming. People not only want your products, but they need them."

The winter passes slowly but pleasantly. Charles enjoys spending time with his daughters and helps me greatly as he continues to convalesce. He tells me he is feeling better every day, but I continue to notice he suffers from headaches, though he never complains.

We become members at Elim Lutheran Church, a Swedish church close to us, and I start studying English on Sunday nights. By now, Charles is fluent in English but goes to a Citizenship Preparation class, as he wants to be well prepared for the citizenship test he will be eligible to take in 1903. When I tell him I think he is way ahead of schedule since 1903 is six years away, he says, "I'm just using my time wisely. I might be way too busy to study in 1903."

As winter is just beginning to lose its hold, and the smell of spring is in the air, Mary is born. Despite the slightest disappointment that she is not a boy, she is welcomed and well-loved. Perhaps overly concerned after losing Anna, I tell Charles I want to take our baby to a doctor because I fear there might be something wrong with her. On a beautiful spring day, with Charles' support, I take Mary in a basket on the wagon into downtown Duluth where I see Dr. Monson, the same doctor who treated Charles after his injury.

He examines the baby carefully and then speaks very seriously: "I'm very sorry to tell you, but your instinct was exactly right. Little Mary is hydrocephalic, which means she has water on her brain. She's beautiful, but her head is a little enlarged. She won't be in any pain, but at some point, probably in a year or two, she will stop thriving and pass away."

The words are incomprehensible. How could this beautiful little girl be so sick? I leave the office in tears, agreeing to bring the baby back when she is a year old. I had planned to see Mrs. G. on the way home to show her little Mary, who has been named after her, but now can only go home to be with Charles, where we both weep over the news. Charles finally says, "We will pray for our daughter. Doctors have been wrong before. We will not give up."

And so our world goes on. We work long days, from sunrise to sunset, and watch our gardens fill with beautiful vegetables. We watch Esther show off all she has learned at school, happily reading to both Hulda and Mary. Hulda is quiet, happy to be read to and even happier with her kitten. The one word, which she clearly says is "Kitty," but that doesn't surprise anyone. After all, Esther talks enough for both of them.

With a newborn and gardens to tend I stop my English lessons, but Esther reads to me, and helps me practice our new language.

Charles is very pleased with how our farm is prospering. He has loyal customers and has no trouble selling all of his milk, butter, cheese and eggs. One forenoon he comes home from his milk route, with a brown bag holding two oranges, two bananas, and several white envelopes. He excitedly gives the fruit to me, telling me he couldn't resist it and then explains the envelopes: "I've been thinking they'd help us with our saving and planning."

I didn't really know what he means until he took out a pencil and began labeling each of them: 1. Church 2. Daily expenses   3. Farm expenses 4. Emergency Fund 5. Future Farm. He takes out the money we have saved and begins dividing it. We keep our savings in a wooden box, locked in my trunk, but now Charles takes money out of it to put in the emergency fund envelope and the rest in the future farm envelope. Then, because we don't know what else to do, he puts both envelopes back in the box and lock it in the trunk.

"Charles, shouldn't we write down somewhere how much we have saved?" He agrees with me, calling me his beautiful business partner. I smile at the compliment and write down each amount at the back of our ledger book. "We need to keep track of the other expenses too, especially the farm expenses."

"You already do that, Elina, in the ledger. We know every dollar we've spent and every dollar we've been paid for our products." We couldn't quite figure out how to keep track of the home expenses, but decide, at the first of the month, to figure out our income, subtract the farm expenses, and put ten per cent of that amount into the church envelope. That way we would be sure to tithe. Charles suggests we put twenty dollars into the living expenses envelope each month, and that would be mine to manage. Rent would eventually take twice that amount, but, until then, if I don't need it all for groceries or items for the family, I can decide whether to put it into the emergency fund, farm savings fund or to buy something special for us. "And you need to have the same privilege, Charles."

"I'll tell you what. If there's something I really need, I will use some of the milk delivery money." He was silent for a moment, but then said, "But I have everything I want and need right here." He looks at me and our children warmly, and I return his smile.

We've come to a point where we almost forget that little Mary has been born with a defect. She is a very contented baby and continues to thrive. I know I'll bring her back to the doctor when she is a year old, but begin to allow myself to believe Dr. Monson might not be correct. In the meantime, I work hard in the garden, and Charles builds a fruit cellar where we can store the vegetables and fruits.

Sundays, after church, we take the buggy up the road to the hills, as far as we can and spend the day picking berries for drying and for making preserves. We stop to enjoy a picnic lunch together, and if the mosquitoes aren't bad, we all take an afternoon nap.

I marvel at my husband, who picks right along with Esther, Hulda and myself. In Sweden berry picking was strictly women's work, but Charles never hesitates to help with any work I do. I've mention how much I appreciate that he does so, and he seems surprised, saying when we married we became one being, so how could it matter who does what chore? I once again marvel that my marriage to Charles is a blessing in ever so many ways.

22

Joy and Sorrow

"And he said, 'Naked I came from my mother's womb, and naked shall I return; the LORD gave, and the LORD has taken away; blessed be the name of the LORD.'"

Job 1:21

July of 1898 marks the first anniversary of Charles' injury. He visits Dr. Monson, who gives him a clean bill of health, telling Charles he is a miracle. His examination of little Mary does not yield as happy a report. When he measures her head, he tells us it is still enlarged due to the extra fluid her brain is holding. He tells us he does not expect to see her alive on her second birthday.

On the ride home, Charles tells me he would trade places with Mary, if only he could, but I reply with painful honesty, "Then I'm truly glad you cannot, for losing Mary will be terrible, but I could not bear losing you."

On July 17, Nathalie Marie is born. We wonder if the good Lord has purposely given her to Charles and me before taking Mary home.

Nathalie thrives while at the same time, Mary weakens gradually and peacefully dies in August. As Charles says, "We need to enjoy the blessings we've been given and make peace with our losses. Someday we'll see Anna, Rosa and Mary in heaven."

It is very difficult for me, but for Charles' and the children's sake I grieve as privately as possible, moving on with my life as best I can. Our pastor visits with me often and even has a woman a little older than me, Margit, who had had a series of miscarriages, visit with me twice. I also seek comfort from my sister Amanda, traveling to her beautiful home with Nathalie and spending two helpful days with her.

The yield of our farm continues to increase, and that fall Charles delivers dairy products Monday through Friday, but then loads the wagon with our whole family and produce on Saturdays, which we sell at a farmers' market. Charles and I had determined long ago that the quality of our products are important to us, and we are rewarded by people seeking them. We use our extra income to surprise Mr. Gundersson by paying him for our first year of rent-free living. As we review our ledger together, Charles and I realize if we continue to do as well as we have been, we should be able to buy our own land in a few years. That realization is a wonderful motivation to both of us.

23

The Arrival of the 20th Century

"Lord, thou hast heard the desire of the humble: thou wilt prepare their heart, thou wilt cause thine ear to hear..."

Psalms 10:17

The arrival of the twentieth century is celebrated in all of Duluth. We marvel at the firework displays both on New Year's Day and on the Fourth of July.

Duluth is forging ahead to beautify the city with the erection of elaborate brick buildings and parks. Churches and schools are being added, along with many beautiful homes, but what excites Charles and me the most is the start of a new Duluth Public Library. The privilege of freely borrowing books to read is a wonderful gift; seeing that it will soon take place in a large and beautiful stone block building is an extra blessing.

On October 7, 1900 I gave birth to the long-awaited first son of the family, who we name Harry William, as we had promised Harry Gundersson we would do.

On October 1, 1902, Charles, after passing his detailed test on American history and government, becomes a United States citizen. He proudly presents his certificate to me, announcing that the children and I are now citizens also. He purchases a frame for the certificate and hangs it proudly by our kitchen table.

On April 20, 1903, I give birth to Victor Emmanuel. Charles tells me he believes God has rewarded me with two healthy sons for giving our little girls over to His care after they had died. His words sting me greatly, and it is the first time I've ever been truly angry with Charles. He'd made it sound as if our two little baby boys make up for losing my little girls. He has no idea what it is like to carry, deliver, and to care for little babes and then to have them die. Whether he could understand it or not, I knew I'd never "get over" the deaths of Anna, Rosa and Mary. I avoid Charles for much of a week, arguing with God all the while, until I am emotionally worn out but have come to a place of peace. Charles and I never again talk of his words, nor did he ever say such a thing again.

Charles and I do feel very blessed to have the family we had always wanted: Esther, at 11, is bright, capable and a great help with the younger children. Hulda, 8, is much more passive and in truth a poor student, but is a great help at home, especially with the animals, with which she is very gentle and seems to favor over people. Nathalie is a happy, busy four-year old, who has a wonderful vocabulary and a very kind disposition. Harry is a busy three-year-old, and now little Victor is a thriving, contented baby. I feel certain there will be no more babies but experience much contentment with our five children.

Charles, also a contented parent, feels it is time to make a move to buying land of our own. Our rented farm is doing well, but with our savings, we are well-equipped to put down money on farmland, and he and I began in earnest to find the perfect spot.

Charles, the children and I sometimes attend the Evangelical Lutheran Church of Midway, the church that our pastor had spoken so fondly of and which had recently been annexed to the Elim church and is served by the same pastor. Amanda and her family belong to the

Midway congregation. After telling members of the congregation we are interested in buying farmland close by, we are soon told of land for sale.

In 1904, we purchase a beautiful parcel of land alongside the north side of the Stark Road just west of the Midway Road. The buildings are not very sturdy: there is a tarpaper-sided house that is ridiculously small for our family of seven, an outhouse, a large, but poorly built barn, and a small chicken coop. It is easy to ignore the poor condition of the buildings, however, in their contrast with beautiful fields and wooded areas. The Midway School borders our farm, and the Midway Lutheran Church is less than a mile away. It will be a wonderful place to raise children and to establish our very own dairy farm. We decide to buy it the same day we first see it, thanking the Lord for the beautiful land to which He has led us.

PART FOUR

The Stark Road Soderberg Farm

"But seek first his kingdom and his righteousness, and all these things will be yours as well."

Matthew 6:33

24

Home Swede Home

"Ask, and it shall be given you, seek and ye shall find; knock, and it shall be opened unto you..."

Matthew 7:7

The move to Midway Township is hard work, as moving always is, but goes smoothly. Once again, I pack our belongings in the wooden crates that I had previously turned into shelving and tables. We do not have a lot of possessions, making packing easy. I look at my trunk, realizing I'd still need to wait to unpack the fine linens packed inside it.

The difficult part is figuring out how to keep the dairy running while moving. We had planned to move the cows a few at a time, behind our wagon, but as the days grow closer to the date we need to vacate our rented home, Charles purchases yet another wagon, this one with high sides that would hold all ten of our cows and would be perfect for hauling hay. We also purchase a second workhorse to pull the heavy wagon.

Charles and I know there will be need for two horses on our farm and try not to think too much about the money we'd spent.

Charles brings the family and a load of household crates on the first trip. After he unloads the crates from the wagon, he returns to Duluth to bring the cows, chickens and cat to their new home.

Esther and I sweep the dust, insects and cobwebs out of the little house. I then scrub it out while Esther and Hulda take over the care of Nathalie, Harry and Victor.

Before I can even finish scrubbing, Charles arrives with the cows. I can tell he is disappointed I have done nothing with the barn in preparation for the evening milking, but he quickly goes to work on that, so he can add fresh hay in preparation for the cows.

The children laugh at how fast their father sweeps and how impatient the cows are to get into the fields. Instead of putting them in the barn, Charles lets down the gate of the wagon, so the cows can walk down and enter a field in which to graze.

While knowing the land is beautiful for a dairy farm, the house has much to be desired. The kitchen is not much more than a lean-to, and the woodstove in it can do little to heat the rest of the house, which is one large room with a loft that is accessed by a wooden ladder. I decide Charles and I will sleep downstairs with the babies while Esther, Hulda and Nathalie can safely use the sleeping loft.

By milking time, Esther, Hulda and I have made new mattresses by filling our old ones with fresh straw, and I have the kitchen organized enough to make pancakes with raspberry sauce and fried eggs. No one complains of the discombobulation in the house. We are simply thankful we have finished moving and that we have food in our bellies.

Charles, Esther and I complete the milking in record time, and, after separating the milk, I fill the clean glass bottles with milk and then others with cream. Once the milk is on ice, and the cows, horses, and chickens are settled in their new homes we all climb onto our freshly filled mattresses and are instantly asleep.

The next morning, after milking, Charles leaves to deliver milk in West Duluth. On the way home he stops in the village of Proctor, adding new customers to his notebook, promising them fresh milk in the morning.

During the next few days, I busy myself with unpacking. I am thankful we have only what we need, so unpacking goes quickly. Once again I convert emptied crates into storage shelves and bedside tables. I don't like my woodstove nearly as much as the old one, but nevertheless have bread baking in it the third day we are in Midway. I also realize that until we make improvements to the kitchen, I cannot have the children near me while I am separating or bottling milk.

With the sun shining brightly I ask Charles and Esther to fill a large tub with water from the pump. I tell them the whole family looks filthy, and I want them all to have a chance to bathe that evening since the next day will be Sunday, and we are definitely attending church.

With the tub secluded behind tall trees and the water in it heated by the sun, I am pleased to be able, with only a small addition of heated water, to bathe Nathalie, Harry, and Victor. I am delighted with the children's plump, healthy bodies, feeling assured these three little beauties will continue to thrive.

I give privacy to Esther and Hulda, so they can bathe, handing them nightgowns to put on and instructing them to brush out each other's hair after shampooing it. Finally, when they emerge from the trees with shining skin and hair, Charles and I fill the tub with more hot water. I bend over the edge of the tub, washing my hair with great glee. We don't both fit in the tub, so we take turns washing each other's backs, luxuriating in the rare experience. "This is wonderful, Charles. The farm is beautiful, and I haven't felt this clean in years." He agrees and after drying off, and putting on night clothes, we return to the farmhouse surprised to find all five of our children sound asleep.

The next day, all shiny clean, and in wrinkled, but clean clothing, we happily walk to the Midway Church, which is conveniently close to our home. On the way, Charles points out the school to Hulda and Esther since they will attend it in the fall, recognizing the wonderful convenience of having school next door.

We had attended the church a few times before we'd moved and were thrilled to be welcomed back by the congregation, by the singing of familiar Swedish hymns, and listening to our beloved pastor from Elim preach. We feel at home amongst a congregation of fellow Swedish farmers. Amanda introduces us to many families with Swedish names: Gulbransons, Thorbergs, Petersons, Starks and Nelsons. She calls us her farmer relatives. Though she obviously means it to be a less than complimentary label, we feel very pleased to be dairy farmers and very welcome. The people, for the most part, live close by and have many positive things to say about our new farm and about our beautiful children. When we leave the church, we feel we have met many potential friends and are pleased with promises they will visit us in the following weeks.

With our busy farm life, we truly do not have time for visitors, but when people stop by, we welcome them. I bake bread every other day and always have coffee on, so, along with our fresh milk and butter, I am continually prepared for visitors. My sister, Amanda and her children Hedvig, Raymond and Anton are the first ones to stop. Amanda's husband, August Hall is a lumberjack, who is gone for most of the spring, summer and fall. The little cousins enjoy each other, but Amanda is not interested in the farm and will not allow her children to enter our ramshackle house. She tells me to come visit her when I need a break from our shack.

Amanda has always enjoyed criticizing me and never hid the fact that she did not approve of Charles. She was clear that she would not settle for the life of a farmer's wife, but I could not see how being married to a lumberjack could be so much better. I have learned to ignore Amanda's comments years ago but still feel sad that I do not have family close by to enjoy. Then I look at Charles and our five children and realize I have a large family right here on our farm that makes up for any conflict with a sister.

25

New Routines on the Stark Road

"And my God will supply every need of yours according to his riches in glory in Christ Jesus. To our God and Father be glory for ever and ever."

Philippians 4:19

By the fall of 1904 we had adjusted well to our new surroundings. Charles and I stretched our savings thin by having a large barn built, replacing the small, rickety one that had been on the farm. By doing so, we know we would be delaying the remodeling of our house by a year or so but feel the sacrifice makes sense. The building of the barn allows us to increase our cow herd to twenty, which we do as soon as the barn is built and stanchions are installed. We had sold vegetables from our gardens in August and would continue doing so through the fall, or whenever they ran out, at a farmers' market in the village of Proctor. While selling our vegetables, we always have our dairy products on display and continually add new customers.

During a rare period when we had an excess of milk, I try my hand at making a few new cheeses. Not only does the family enjoy them, but our milk customers order the new cheeses also.

When school starts for Esther and Hulda, it is a big adjustment for me to no longer have the girls to watch Nathalie, Harry and Victor. Much to my surprise, Nathalie, a very mature five-year-old seems more than willing to care for her little brothers, especially while I am working with the milk.

When Charles notices how dangerous it is for me to have the children underfoot while working in the kitchen with the separating, bottling and cheese making, as well as my other cooking and baking tasks, he asks me if I would like him to make a fenced area in the yard in which the children could safely play while the weather remains warm enough. I am appreciative that he is even aware of the difficulty I am having and even more appreciative when he completes a simple structure. Charles adds a small pile of sand, and the boys play inside their huge play area while Nathalie plays with them and I watch from the kitchen windows. During the unusually mild month of September, the system works well, but when cold weather begins in the middle of October the children move inside.

Charles, Esther, and I milk before the other children wake. We leave the milk in covered pails outside while everyone has breakfast at the kitchen table. When it is done, Esther helps her father load the bottled milk on the wagon, and Nathalie and Hulda watch the boys in our bedroom, since the little ones cannot be in the kitchen while the milk is being processed. Charles carries in the pails of milk, putting them on the table, and tells Hulda he is ready to leave. He kisses me good-bye and takes Esther, Hulda and their lunch boxes to school. It would be a short walk, but Hulda easily becomes sidetracked, and if he drives them in the buggy, he is sure she is on time.

I empty the milk, one pail at a time, into the separator, putting gallon jars under the milk and cream spouts, and then turn the crank which allowed the cream to be separated from the milk by centrifugal force. After each pail is separated I'd pour the milk into the glass bottles I had washed and rinsed in boiling water the night before. Once capped, I write the date on and put the bottles in the icebox. There are usually forty gallons of milk in the morning and thirty gallons in the evening. Mondays, since it is already processed, Charles takes a large supply of milk with him, but Tuesday through Friday, usually comes home to get a second load of milk to deliver after I've had time to bottle it. Either way, he comes home by noon for lunch, unloading the empty bottles and, on most days, ice for the ice boxes.

Charles visits with the children while I put a simple lunch on the table. There is always bread and cheese and usually apples or dried berries. Nathalie often has stories of the antics of her brothers and Charles always had something to tell us about a customer or two or something he has seen.

With lunch over, Harry and Victor are put down for naps, and Nathalie is given the free time she needs, during which she usually chooses to accompany her father to check on the cows, muck out the barn, feed the chickens and gather their eggs. He adds hay to the feed holders in the barn, carries in water, and has the barn set for the evening. If there are vegetables to harvest, Charles, with Nathalie's help, does that also, so I can wash them before nightfall.

On a rare day, Charles and I, after starting our day before sunrise, take a short nap before Esther and Hulda return from school, eager for a snack and to talk about their day. I attempt to dedicate the next hour of the day to the children before milking and milk processing chores start once again. Sometime during the day I put a soup or stew on for our supper, or prepare fish or eggs while Charles and Esther milk the cows.

During my week I fit in scrubbing the house, tending the garden, mending, and sewing simple garments for our daughters. Because of the tragic accident of one of Amanda's sons falling into hot laundry water, I switch to doing laundry on Saturday mornings when Esther and Hulda can supervise their younger siblings. Charles and I work very hard every day, for that is life on a dairy farm, and we are never caught up with what we want to get done, but we love the Lord, each other, and our children, and feel a deep contentment.

LINDA A. HATINEN

On a rare moment, usually while doing morning milking, we talk about the farmhouse we will build someday. We have the spot picked out for it, slightly closer to the Stark Road than our current house, amongst beautiful, mature trees. We plant lilac shrubs also, so the house will be surrounded by them on all but the north side. We also plan the changes we will make to our current house to make it more comfortable. Charles comes to the conclusion he'd need to hire help for the summer, so he could tend to gardens and do the haying, which is so very necessary to feed the cows. There are always fences that need to be repaired, wood to be cut and split for our wood stove, rocks to be removed, and on and on it goes. The children, however, are thriving and make everything worth it. Though our house is crowded, it is full of love and laughter. Charles and I enjoy watching our little ones run and play.

Sunday, inasmuch as possible, remains a day of rest. Of course the cows have to be milked and the milk bottled, but, as I had learned to do early on in our marriage, I try to get cooking chores started on Saturday, so the family can relax and have fun together. We all go to church and Sunday School, realizing the church is not only our place of spiritual nourishment but our place for socializing. Charles usually plans an adventure for the afternoon. Often we picnic in the woods or fields, but more often we eat a good meal inside, and then load the wagon with hay, on which the children sit and hitch up the horses, so we can visit neighbors, or even ride into Duluth. The children love going to Duluth and are in awe of the large buildings they consider to be castles. Sometimes we go along the shores of Lake Superior, where all of us search for rocks or driftwood to collect, and sometimes, especially when weather is not conducive to travel, we stay at home playing games or listening to Charles read or tell his wonderful stories, some true sand some wonderful fantasy.. On Sundays we all have a chance to nap in order to revive ourselves for the following week.

In 1905, Charles hires a carpenter from our congregation to fix up our little home. We need more room and just a little more comfort. We plan within ten years to build a new home, so we don't want to put a lot of money into what we call our "little house". Together with the carpenter we decide to make the kitchen as wide as the rest of the house. A pantry is added, and a wall partitioned off Charles' and my bedroom from the all-purpose living room. A stairway is added to the loft, an additional stove is purchased and another chimney added. He finishes the ceilings and inner walls and adds a porch leading to the kitchen. Finally, he covers the house with wood siding, which he paints white. Our house has been converted into a functional, cozy home.

On the thirteenth of December, I surprise the family with a St. Lucia Day celebration. That morning, Esther dressed all in white and wearing a crown of candles, which had come to America in my emigrant trunk, serves her brothers and sisters fancy cookies I had found time to make. They included rolled out sugar cookies, pepparkokkar, which were crispy and spicy, and rolled krumkake. Then she brings coffee to Charles and me and warm cocoa to Nathalie, Harry and even little Victor. While everyone eats the special treats, Charles tells the children about St. Lucia, who had lived on the island of Sicily hundreds of years earlier. Because the Christians were being persecuted for their faith, they hid in catacombs or caves that were very dark. Wearing a crown of candles on her head so she could see, Lucia brought bread to feed the hungry Christians. Charles was especially touched by my surprise, telling me the celebration was one of the few memories he had of his mother and thought his time living in Mrs. G's boarding house would be the last time he would be able to celebrate the special Swedish holiday. Esther, who was learning about world geography asked why the Swedes celebrated something that happened in Sicily. Neither Charles nor I had an answer. Little Nathalie had a good response when she said, "Well, I'm glad the Swedes do celebrate something that happened so far away. I helped Mother with the cookies, you know."

School was out for two weeks for Christmas vacation, which was a great relief to me. I had started making gifts for all of the children but was running out of time. Now, I could be busy at the treadle sewing machine while Esther and Hulda took over other jobs, mostly supervising Harry and Victor.

For the first time, during our marriage, Charles and I decide to have a Christmas tree in our home. With a woods full of evergreens,

Charles, Esther, and Hulda choose the perfect tree to cut down. They set it in a corner of our living room, and it fills the house with a wonderful woodsy scent. The only other smells to compete with it are the wonderful aromas coming from the baking we are doing. I needed to replace the cookies that had been devoured on Lucia Day and added deep-fried fattigman and rosettes, cookies that Charles and I had not had since leaving Sweden. Nathalie was my chief helper. She watches my every step and announces she "wants to be a baker when she gets big." Charles and I want our children to have good educations and already have "savings envelopes" started for Esther and Hulda.

Esther is determined to decorate the tree like the one at school, and though I won't allow her to have candles on the tree, I enjoy having the girls make ornaments from paper, pinecones and bits of ribbons.

The house takes on an air of festivity and happiness. The younger children are puzzled by packages that appear under the tree. Wise Esther and Hulda tell them all about Jesus' birth and how people gave gifts to one another to remember the three kings who brought gifts to baby Jesus.

On the Sunday before Christmas the children are to be in a Sunday School program at the Midway Lutheran Church. That morning we walk to church, while pulling Victor and Harry on a toboggan. I was the last one in line, making sure the little boys don't tumble from the sled and are left behind. We are all bundled in our warmest clothes, and the morning is beautiful with huge snowflakes falling on everyone.

The program is after the beautiful service. The children, usually well behaved, are almost too excited to sit. When the service is over, capable Esther leads the children downstairs, where they put on costumes. Victor falls asleep in my arms, but Harry stands on the pew looking at the back of the church for his sisters to return.

Finally, the organ starts playing, and candles in each window are lit. The children march up, and Harry excitedly waves and calls out to Esther, Hulda and Nathalie as they seriously march up to the front of the church with their classes, shushing their embarrassing little brother. Each class has a part in the pageant. Nathalie's class of girls are dressed as angels, and their pure, untrained singing voices fit their costumes perfectly.

Hulda's and Esther's classes say "pieces", telling the story of Jesus' birth. By the end, the congregation is as joyful as the children. Little bags of fruit and candies are handed out to the children, and even Victor and Harry are given one to carry home.

The next week is one of secrets and mysteries. Charles, Esther, and Hulda take over as much of the barn work as possible, leaving me to continue my gift making. Charles continues his deliveries, even on Christmas Eve Day, sometimes staying away longer than I think his route should take, but I don't ask any questions.

Despite the excitement, Hulda becomes inconsolable because her dear old cat, "Kitty", has been found dead in the yard. No one can explain what has happened, and she cries in the arms of Charles and me until I can't believe she has any tears left. Charles tells her that Jesus knows the cat has died, and now He will take care of it. Esther interrupts, saying "That's not true. Only people have souls...."

Charles shushes his oldest daughter, thinking she sometimes knows too much. When Hulda asks her father if that was true, he says, "I think it is, child, but that's why God made kind, kind people like you to take care of animals on earth. It hurts to say good-bye, but just remember what a good time Kitty had on earth, and how good you were to her. Hulda finally stops crying but is very serious until Christmas Eve Day, when curiosity over the packages overcomes even her blues.

That evening we eat a festive dinner after the milking is done. We follow the traditions we'd observed in Sweden, celebrating with lutefisk, a dried cod fish that is rehydrated and cooked, served with melted butter, meatballs, our own boiled potatoes, carrots and rutabagas as well as a wonderful assortment of breads, including rye, oatmeal and a delectable cardamom bread, flavored with the spice that I had brought with me from Sweden. Before dessert, I clear the table and surprise everyone by delaying dish washing and instead ushering the family into the living room to listen to Charles read the Christmas story and then open gifts. Each child has two gifts to open: one from their Swedish grandfather and one that I had made. The ones from Sweden are opened to reveal wooden trucks for Harry and Victor, a doll for Nathalie, and books for Esther and Hulda. My father has also sent a beautiful photo of Ljungsjömåla, which I will proudly hang on the wall. I had made dresses for Esther, Hulda, and Nathalie along with matching bags for Esther and Hulda and a rag doll with a matching dress for Nathalie. I had knitted mittens for Charles, Harry and Victor.

Charles surprised the family with wonderful gifts he had shopped for and which even I had not known about. He smiles mischievously at me as he brings in gifts he'd put in the entryway after milking. He has teddy bears for Victor and Harry. The boys squeal in delight at their new toys. He gives Nathalie a box with crayons, colored pencils, and paper, which Nathalie hugs with joy. He gives three books to Esther, with the condition that he wants to read them also. She smiles at her father's understanding of exactly what she likes.

"Oh dear," Charles says suddenly. "Did I forget Hulda and Mother? Esther, will you help me?" She smiles, conspiratorially, and hurries to the barn, where she retrieves a beautiful cat, who even wears a ribbon.

Hulda cries with happiness as she talks to and pets her new cat.

Then Charles and Esther carry a wash stand into the living room. I watch in dismay as they assemble it. A wringer is in the center and platforms pull out on each side. Esther explains how I will have wash water in a tub on one side and rinse water on the other. After being washed I'll put the clean clothes through the wringers, turning the crank to squeeze out the water. I did not even know such a convenience existed and am thrilled to think how much effort and time will be saved by using it. Just when I think there could be no more happiness, Charles goes outside once more, returning with an adorable little brown puppy. The children cannot believe their eyes as they look at the little dog. After everyone has had a turn to hold the little guy, Charles wisely puts him in his box where he can have some peace.

Then there is rice pudding and cookies for anyone who wants it along with candy canes Charles has brought home. The children are all delighted, but not as much as Charles and I am. I look at Charles with pure love as he takes me in his arms and kisses me. The children, not used to seeing such affection displayed by their parents, clap for us. Charles and I, red-faced but very pleased, can only laugh.

That Christmas was the first time Charles had freely spent money on anything but essentials. He told me that many of his customers had given him money that they called "tips" during the past week to thank him for his good products and good service. He tells me he has never bought a gift for anyone before that Christmas, and now that he knows how good it feels to buy something for someone, he wants to keep doing it. It was one of those moments when I again realize the disparity between Charles' and my backgrounds. We talk long into the night as we r wash and put away the supper dishes. I learn for the first time that there were many times when Charles hadn't even had enough to eat. He also talks about being teased by children about his raggedy clothes. Before falling asleep he says, "Elina, I have so very much. It is like a dream come true, and best of all, I have you and the children"

There was an early Christmas morning church service, Julotta, which started at five, but the children were all sound asleep, and after milking, Charles wisely suggested we all stay home. It was a good decision for our happy family, who spent the day playing with their new puppy, who had been named Star, and the new kitten, Mittens. The puppy and kitten, worn out from all of the attention, fell asleep together, which started a lifelong friendship between the two animals.

26

Continued Growth

"Commit your works to the LORD, and your plans will be established."

Proverbs 16:5

Charles liked to say that everything grew well on our farm, including our family. Herbert Isaiah was born in 1906 and Ruth was born in 1907. I felt certain that, at the age of 39, Herbert and Ruth would be our last children. Somehow that made them all the more precious to both Charles and to me.

For Christmas, 1907, Charles surprised us all with a record player. He showed us how he put a disc on the spindle, set the needle into a groove, and turn the crank. The children were amazed that music came out of the box. They watch the record spin and think it is magic. Charles tells them about many new inventions, including electricity, horseless carriages, telephones, and radios. He tells them they will all grow up experiencing such things, and many more. The children looked at him in amazement, and I marvel at how much he knows about the world.

With our family of seven children, Charles and I began seriously planning our farm house. We'd had a milk house built where the milk was separated, bottled, and stored on ice, but I still wanted a large kitchen where the children could play while I cooked. We asked the man who had remodeled our old house to come visit us, so we could talk about house plans, and while all three of us talked together, Mr. Lawson, the carpenter, sketched plans on a large piece of a brown paper bag with a pencil. The main floor had a huge kitchen, a pantry, a dining room, parlor and one small bedroom. Mr. Lawson added a back entry and large front porch at our request. Then together we planned four bedrooms upstairs, so there would be a room for Charles and me, for Esther and Hulda, for Nathalie and Ruth, and for the boys, Harry, Victor and Herbert. Esther was already fifteen and attending high school, but we felt with space planned for all, the children would always feel welcome to return home. Mr. Lawson talked about an open stairway and many built-in cabinets. He said he would determine how much it would cost and get back to us. At church the next Sunday, Lawson handed Charles an envelope, and we eagerly opened it after walking home. He told us the house would cost close to six thousand dollars to build, and that he could start once we had two thousand dollars saved to cover building materials. He mentioned the possibility of building the basement and first floor in one year and finishing the upstairs the next year. Charles had read about mortgages but didn't want to go into debt. Together we pored over our ledger books and felt confident we could start the house in 1910. We tacked the house drawings on one of our living room walls as a reminder of the plans we had. Charles had hoped to hire a farmhand but decided not to, so he could save more money for our house.

Esther wants to attend nurses' training at St. Luke's Hospital in Duluth or attend the Normal School to prepare for teaching, and Charles and I are determined to make that possible in 1910 when she would graduate from high school. Hulda, three years younger, shows no interest in further school. Her teachers described her as slow, and I suspect she will want to stay at the farm. She has a wonderful way with the animals and is a good help in the barn. Nathalie is growing up to be a big help both inside and out. I once told Charles I sometimes feel guilty at how much Nathalie did in the house. She is a good student, but loves to take over cooking or baking for me, as well as to watch the younger children. She does not mind work outside, but obviously has a heart for work in the kitchen. The three boys, Harry, Victor and Herbert are not in school yet and love running and playing outside or in, and little Ruth has no choice but to be contented watching the commotion of her brothers and sisters. Nathalie enjoys taking care of her, and I often think how wise God was to create breast milk since feeding time is the one time I am able to completely concentrate on beautiful little Ruth.

Charles' number of customers continue to grow in number and satisfaction. The twenty cows we have are good producers, and he sometimes has extra milk to sell to Bridgeman's, a dairy processor in Duluth, but we realize his profit is much higher when he sells products directly to customers. With the milk house in operation he also has customers stop at the farm to buy milk, cream, cheese, and even vegetables during the summer and fall. He is proud of our accomplishments and feels it is good for me to meet customers. He seems to feel I need more ways in which to socialize.

On Tuesdays, Charles spends an extra hour in town, buying feed for his cows and chickens, and shopping for whatever else is needed at the farm. At least once a month, he encourages me to accompany him for errands even if it means we can't leave until the girls come home from school. A quick trip to the sundries store in Proctor satisfies my need to pick out fabrics and notions for sewing, and a stop at the grocery store is the source for the few food items we need to buy.

In 1908, Charles visits a bank for the first time and learns about loans, mortgages and insurance. He comes home telling me he still doesn't want to go into debt, but will start the house, knowing he can borrow if he absolutely needs to. He also tells me about insurance, a concept that is incomprehensible to me.

During the winter, my periods are irregular, and I believe I am entering a new season of life, menopause. After all, I am thirty-nine. I also am very tired, which I'd heard could be a symptom of menopause also. There is never time to rest, especially during the spring and summer months, when crops need tending, hay cut and stacked, and fences repaired. Much to my surprise in early spring, I realize my "menopause" is in fact a pregnancy. My tall frame hides the growing baby, and everyone at church is surprised after I deliver a baby boy that May. Our baby is fine featured with blonde hair. His translucent skin reminds me of a china doll I'd once seen. I secretly believe he is the most beautiful baby I'd ever seen. Charles and I name our precious boy Hjalsuar Laureutius, after a third century martyred saint I'd read about in a novel. The fanciful, but beautiful name, seems perfect for our beautiful son. Charles goes along with the name as long as he could call him Laurence, the name we'd planned on if we had another boy. Knowing he truly is my last baby, I look for excuses to rock him in the rocking chair and count every time I breast feed him to be a blessing.

That fall Esther turns sixteen years old. She thinks it is somehow disgraceful that her "old mother" should have yet another baby. Hulda is 12 and begins high school with limited success. Nathalie is a responsible nine-year-old, who takes over many of the kitchen duties, while I take care of Laurence. Our "wild boys", as we call them, are six, four, and two. They are good boys but are on the move all day. While Harry and Victor are at school, Herbert tries to convert toddler Ruth into a rowdy boy but has no success.

In the summer, whooping cough sweeps through Midway and consequently our household, including all of the children plus me. Only Charles escapes the illness since he had experienced it as a child. The sound of the deep cough fills our house for weeks, as one by one we fall prey to the disease. Finally, the cough only remains in Laurence and me. When he realizes how extremely run down I am, Charles asks Esther to stay home from her first week of school to tend to Laurence and to me. During that time of caring for us, Esther not only did a wonderful job but announces she will definitely study to become a nurse.

On the night of September 7, I finally felt relief because Laurence is not experiencing the wracking cough any more. I wake the following morning, pleased that Laurence had been able to sleep through the night. Charles finds me an hour later rocking Laurence in the rocking chair. "Elina, is something wrong?" he asks, wondering why I wasn't making breakfast for the family. "We're done milking."

I remember looking at him hopelessly and finally saying, "It's our baby. He's dead."

Not wanting to believe me, he puts his finger to our baby's neck but can't detect a pulse. "I will go to the gas station," he says, "and phone the funeral home. I don't know what else to do."

"Let the pastor know—and my sister, but come back soon. The children and I need you."

He runs to the gas station that is at the corner of the Midway and Stark Roads and makes the phone calls, and then he returns home to the house that is too quiet and too dark.

The pastor arrives first and prays with Charles and me. We hear the words once again: God knows our pain and will be with us. He also suggests that a funeral be held two days later at the church. He stays with us until the mortician arrives, many hours later. He extends his sympathies and then takes our little boy out of my arms. It feels to me as if he were ripping out my heart. He speaks softly and gently as he asks for clothes for our little boy to be buried in and details for the service. I say nothing so Charles gives as much information as he can, asking that "Children of the Heavenly Father" and "Jesus Loves Me" be sung. The mortician asks us to go to West Duluth later in the day to select a casket, but Charles, looking at me, asks the mortician to choose for us-- something simple and small for our little boy.

After the men have left, Charles asks Nathalie to make some supper while he helps the children get dressed. At six and nine, Victor and Harry have many questions: "Where did the man take Laurence?", "Why had he died?" and "What would happen to him now?"

Charles patiently answers the questions as best he can, hugging the boys and wiping away their tears and his own. Meanwhile, I sit quietly. Charles hugs me also, and finally I break into the tears that I've been holding back. After a long cry, I say, "I can't bear this Charles. This is the fourth baby I've delivered that has died. It's too painful for me."

Charles simply says, "It's too much for anyone to bear. We can't handle our loss, so let God handle it for us."

"Oh, my Charles, I can't do this again."

"Don't try, Elina. Just know that as the pastor said, 'God is with us.' Remember, He lost his own son on the cross. He knows exactly how we're feeling, and he'll help us recover."

"I can't figure out why He's given us these four babies, only to take them back. It's too cruel."

"But we know God isn't cruel, so it must be that we aren't able to understand."

"Have some food, Elina. You need to eat." I follow him to the table and eat a few tasteless spoonsful of soup and have a few swallows of coffee. It isn't much, but Charles is relieved to see me take a step forward.

The next day neighbors stop by to give us their condolences and usually a dish of food besides. Charles makes his milk route and does his barn work. He checks on me frequently, encouraging me any way he can. He also talks with Hulda and Nathalie, thanking them for their help. Esther takes charge of everyone and has the house clean and everyone, even me, looking spic and span. Amanda comes with a ham and sits with me for hours.

And then there is the funeral. I don't notice much of what is going on. Instead I gaze at the little casket, holding my precious Laurence. Before the casket has been closed I look at his body one last time, once again believing he is the most beautiful baby I've ever seen.

The church ladies serve a lunch of sandwiches and cookies, and people visit after the service with cups of coffee and their food. I am surprised by how many people have come: neighbors, church members, plus Mrs. G and her brother-in-law, Harry, who talks at length not only with Charles and me but with his namesake, little Harry, who is surprised that such an important looking man would spend time with him.

The casket is buried in the church cemetery in a lot that Charles has chosen. It is shaded by a huge oak tree. We stay at the cemetery for a while and then start walking home. Before we even make it onto the Midway Road, Amanda's husband, August, stops with his new Model T and picks up Ruth and me, driving us home. I thank August for his kindness and then go into the empty house with Ruth in my arms. Within minutes the rest of the family has returned, excited about the Model T, asking me questions I have no interest in answering. Instead, I excuse myself and leave to take a nap. Charles comes into the bedroom to change out of his church clothes and to put his farming clothes back on.

"It was a nice service, didn't you think, Elina?"

"Ya, I suppose so.......thank you for making all of the arrangements, especially choosing the beautiful cemetery plot."

"You're welcome, dear. Now rest. We'll take care of the house and farm without you for a few days or as long as you need."

"All right," I say as my heavy eyes close. Charles removes my shoes and covers me with a blanket. I think he should remove my dress clothes also, but it doesn't really matter. Nothing matters.

Esther has asked for three more days off from school to assist us, so she takes charge and keeps everyone but me busy. Since she'd decided to become a nurse, she's become fanatic about cleanliness and has things scrubbed inside and out. She also insists that I get up for meals and go outside for air each afternoon. I hear her tell Charles that whatever he does, he couldn't let me stay in bed all day. I obey her strict orders but realize no matter what she makes me do, she can't change what I am thinking.

I feel as if a black, black curtain is covering me.

By the time Esther goes back to school, the rest of the family is relieved. The children secretly call her "the general". The children know that the house and farm are in good order, but they have grown tired of her bossiness, especially Nathalie, who is used to working hard but not having someone check her work so closely.

On Monday, all of the children but Hebert and Ruth go back to school. Charles milks the cows with the help of Hulda and then processes the milk himself. I'm sure he hopes I will be able to get the children dressed and fed, and with Nathalie's help I do. As usual, Charles takes the children to school before delivering milk; then he goes on his way to Proctor and West Duluth, returning home in record time.

He finds me sitting in my rocker, watching Herbert and Ruth play in the kitchen. I haven't started anything for lunch, but the icebox is filled with sandwiches, canned fruit and lemonade and tins of cookies cover the counter, so Charles puts things on the table. As he is pouring glasses of milk, I say "Since you're home I'm going to bed."

Charles pauses for a moment and finally says, "Elina, the children and I need you. I don't mean to sound cruel, but you can't exercise the luxury of grieving while the children are untended and unfed. You'll have to limit your grieving to while they're sleeping."

I look at him first with empty eyes, then a flash of anger, but finally say, "I know you're right." I move out of the chair and into Charles' arms and say, "Please, be careful. I couldn't bear to lose you too."

"Hush, Elina. I'm strong and healthy. The Lord will look out for us all."

I'm sure the Lord was looking after us, but I couldn't sense it. I couldn't even imagine it. I'd had enough with a god who ripped babies out of my arms. If He could have prevented it, I believed He was cruel not to have done so. If He couldn't prevent it, then of what use was He?

A few days later, Charles told me he'd asked Dr. Monson to come see me. I didn't have any idea what he could do, but it was easier simply to go along with Charles' plans than to resist. After all, it would have done no good. Dr. Monson came the next day to examine me, and I became close to hysterical: He couldn't see what was going on in my mind. He couldn't even move the curtain that continued to cover me.

I heard Dr. Monson and Charles outside our bedroom talking. The doctor told Charles that "Between the stress of losing Laurence, still recovering from whooping cough and probably the beginning of menopause, she's in a deep depression. I suggest you have her hospitalized."

Something came undone in me when I heard those words. I could not and would not be separated from Charles and our children. A wee corner of the curtain lifted, and I got out of bed. Going into the kitchen, I said in a scratchy, unused voice, "I do not need a hospital. I need to be with my family and I will be all right." I was so weak that I nearly fell to the floor, but Charles helped me to our bed, and the doctor left pills and some kind of a tonic, which Esther gave to me faithfully each day. The hopelessness and lethargy lasted for many, many months, but I knew I could not leave my family desolate, so somehow, despite sorrow and loss, I moved on. In talking to Amanda, I said there were four holes in my heart where Anna, Rosa, Mary and Laurence had been, but I knew there was too much to do to indulge in crying away days at a time.

Amanda, having lost two children herself, understood my sorrow, and was a big help to me once again. For weeks she came to stay with me every day while Charles delivered milk. Both Amanda and I realize our husbands do not want to hear our sad thoughts, so we confide in each other and bravely carry on with life. Any differences we'd had in the past dissolve in our tears. Once again, we are each other's confidantes and closest friend.

Charles starts talking more about the house we are going to build and even traces out its shape in the grass, putting sticks in at each corner. I suspect he does it as a distraction for my pain, and even though I'm not interested in a new house, I pretend I am. Charles tells me he has talked with the builder, and he'll be ready to start in the fall of the following year, 1910.

Though I continue to grieve, I do it very privately. Sometimes when tears surprise me, I weed for a while or scrub until the tears stop. The kitchen tables and woodstove have never been so clean. All the while, we continue to have a wonderful yield of produce in our gardens. Charles has also planted both raspberries and strawberries in patches close to our house, so I have easy access to them.

Always looking for ways to get me out of the house, one day Charles tells me he would like me to go on his route a few times, so I know what he does and where his customers live. To please him, on a September morning, I bundle Herbert and Ruth and climb on the wagon with them to join Charles. He makes the morning fun for the children, as he makes his stops first in Proctor and later in West Duluth. He brings out a ball for the children to use while they ride, and they happily throw it into a bushel basket on the wagon, sing songs, and look at books he's taken with for them.

I am surprised by all of the customers and how well Charles knows them. He is consistently friendly, asking thoughtful questions, and introducing the children and me whenever a customer comes out to the wagon.

All the while he shows me how he records what he delivers and how he notes how much is owed and when it is paid. It actually is a simple system, especially since the address and "standing order" are listed on each card.

At one stop, a gentleman is just leaving the house, and after dropping off the milk, I hear Charles say, "I haven't paid anything to you this month." He then hands the fellow a dollar, and they shake hands.

"Who is that Charles, and why did you give him money?"

He answers, "He's the Aid to Lutherans man."

I have no understanding of what he's said and am immediately sidetracked by a rare squabble between Herbert and Ruth. Charles tells the children there are only two stops left and then he has a surprise for them. They are very cooperative for the two stops, and then together ask "What's the surprise?"

Instead of answering, Charles pulls up to a grocery school, where I pick out a few oranges and bananas, wonderful treats for the family while Charles takes the children to the candy counter where they choose lollipops for themselves and for their brothers and sisters. With each carrying a small sack, they happily climb onto the wagon and then intently lick their lollipops all the way home.

One day in 1909 Charles came home from his milk route excited to tell me he's learned from one of his customers that land adjacent to ours is going to be put up for sale. It is wonderful pasture land and would be a good addition to our farm. As we look over our savings, we know that by purchasing it, we will have to delay the building of our house. The land purchase would require the use of both our house and emergency fund, and money would be tight until we built up an emergency fund again. After talking and praying we go ahead and purchase the land. That evening the whole family walks to the land we've purchased, which is shaped like a triangle. One of the sides is adjacent to the Midway River, and the boys began making plans to fish. Now we own adjacent land that faces the Midway Road, the Stark Road Stark Junction Road and the Midway River.

"Look how beautiful it is here, Elina. Some day one of our children or grandchildren will build a house on this land."

"It is very beautiful, and good grazing land, but what about our house?" I ask.

"I promise you the house will be built," he solemnly replies, "just later than we'd planned."

27

Peace Returns and Is Interrupted

"Pray at all times, with all prayer and supplication. To that end keep alert with all perseverance, making supplication for all the saints...."

Ephesians 6:18

Somehow, over the months, we continued with our life. As we grieved in silence, Charles and I became closer, something I didn't think was even possible. And finally, my anger with God disappeared. We were careful to keep our sadness from our children, wanting to protect them. We made a promise to each other that even though we needed to work hard and desired to save money for our new home, we would do something together each Sunday to help build family memories, something that Charles had never had.

So winter came with skating on the Midway River and tobogganing down the hills. Charles made skis for the children, and they skied all over the farm. He also took us on adventures to Duluth with stops at the huge, beautiful library to check out books and a ride on the Incline, a motorized car that went up the hill and back down for a nickel for each rider. The children loved it, and so did Charles and I. When spring came, Charles learned how to play baseball right along with Harry and Victor and went fishing for brook trout in the Midway River. We had several brook trout meals, and the boys always had tales of the big one that got away. We resumed going for hikes in our woods, seeing who could spot the first wild flowers. The more we explored our land, the more beautiful we found it to be.

At the same time, it was obvious to me that Charles was not feeling well. His headaches had returned, and he had no appetite. He was losing weight, but his hands and feet were swollen. I learned after the fact that not wanting to alarm me Charles secretly made an appointment with Dr. Monson. Afterwards, Charles told me that Dr. Monson greeted him warmly. The two visited for a bit, and when he asked about me, Charles told him that the loss of Laurence still bothered me, but that I seemed to be managing. Dr. Monson suggested I make an appointment too, but then he took Charles' history, and his attention was clearly focused on him. When asked about his health history Charles remembered he could not enlist in the Swedish Army due to having something in his urine. Dr. Monson sent a urine sample to the lab, and when Charles returned to the doctor's office three days later, the results had come back, and the doctor told him he had Bright's disease, a kidney disease with which he'd probably been born. He told him that eventually his kidneys would stop working altogether, but in the meantime, he would be given medication to help him live as normal a life as possible. Before leaving, Charles asked the question he most badly wanted answered, "How much time do I have?"

The doctor answered, "No one can know for sure, but if you take good care of yourself, I suspect you could easily live another ten years.... but I don't expect you to reach sixty." Charles knew he had to prepare me for his death. As he slowly rode home he thought of what he would tell me, and then decided on another quick stop, where he purchased a set of plain, gold wedding rings, one for him and one for me.

When he came home, I was upset that he was so late. It had been the last day of school, and the children were overly excited and very rambunctious. Hulda was upset about something, but would not tell me what it was, and Nathalie, who was such a faithful helper, had stomach flu and was in bed.

Later that afternoon Charles told me his bad news, but first he told the boys to play outside and to watch Herbert and Ruth. Then he asked me what needed to be done for supper, and I said soup was bubbling, and we'd have bread and cheese with it. Seeing how tired I was, he told me to take a nap, while he set the table and sliced cheese and my rye bread. He checked on Nathalie, who said her stomach hurt, and she had "runs." She told her father she had come home early from school after vomiting. She seemed more upset about missing the end of her school year than about being sick. He held her little shoulders as she cried against him, and then tucked her in. He prayed with her, asking Jesus to heal her and then left to check the soup, which he tasted and felt was ready, and then checked on Hulda, who had been moody of late. He found her in the barn, talking to her cat, and when he asked her what was wrong, she told him the teacher said she could not go onto her next year of high school. "She said my reading and writing and math are all worse than a little child. She hates me."

"Let me see your report card, Hulda." She pulled it out of her pocket, and when Charles saw it, he realized Hulda's perceptions had been accurate. He didn't know what she had told Hulda, but the teacher had written "I cannot in good conscience recommend that Hulda go on to another year of high school. Her skills are not at the level where she could possibly have success."

Charles and I knew that Hulda was slow, but she was a hard worker in the barn and had many good traits. Later, Charles told me he explained, "It's all right Hulda. God made us all different. For some reason he made it difficult for you to learn school subjects, so He must have a special job for you to do." He told me she looked at him with such trust that he felt unfit to be a father. "Let's go inside, Hulda. Help me round up the children."

He gave a whistle, and five little ones ran to him, asking him if they could play one more round of Hide and Seek. He agreed, as long as he could be it, and that once they were caught, they quietly went inside, washed up for supper, and sat down at the table." He asked Hulda to go inside to make sure the children followed his directions. The children were delighted and hid while their father counted to thirty. When he opened his eyes, he "found" Ruth standing at his feet, looking up at him with a huge, beautiful smile.

One by one he found the boys: Victor was up in a tree, Harry was curled up in the barn, and Herbert was hidden in a hay pile. They were cooperative about going in, especially as their father congratulated them on their "excellent hiding places." Hulda had poured milk, and after washing, Charles dished up soup, so it would cool for the little ones. Only then did he gently wake me and check on Nathalie, who remained sound asleep.

Supper went unusually well. I handled the cleanup, grateful for the rest Charles had given me. I was revived, and joined him for the evening milking. Almost immediately I asked him why he had been so very late, unaware of the significance of my question.

"I've been feeling a little under the weather, so I finally checked in with Dr. Monson."

When he didn't give a further explanation, I finally blurted, "So did you find out what is going on?"

I don't think he'd planned to give me all the information while we did the milking, but there was no way to make me wait now, so he finally answered, "I have Bright's disease. It's a problem with my kidneys."

I nodded, and then asked, "How serious is it?"

"It's serious, Elina. People can't live without kidneys, and mine are wearing out."

"Do you mean you're dying?" I whispered.

"Elina, I asked the doctor the same question, and he said I could live ten years, but probably won't make my sixtieth birthday, but he also said no one can ever be sure."

"How do you feel, Charles? You never complain."

"I haven't felt wonderful. That's why I went to see the doc. I've had backaches, and my headaches have come back. You've noticed I've lost weight, and lately I'm tired way before I should be. The doctor gave me some medicine, so I won't have so much fluid in my hands and feet. Other than that, we just need to pray."

I didn't say anything, but Charles could tell that I was thinking over everything he'd said.

We brought the milk to the milk house, separated and bottled it, talking about many things but not his disease.

He told me Hulda's sad news and said the more he thought about it, he'd like her to go to agriculture school. "I suspect she'll always want to work on our farm, so let's give her some education for it."

"Esther's nurses' training will be for three years. Will we have enough money to pay for both schools?"

"You've seen the numbers. After all, you're the one who keeps the books. We're doing well."

"And what about the house?"

"I've told you we will build the house."

He heard my deep sigh, but I didn't complain. "Elina, forgive me, please. I made a purchase today that wasn't exactly a necessity."

Hearing that at such a critical time, I wanted to lash out in anger, but instead finally asked "So what did you buy?"

He reached into his pocket and pulled out a small velvet bag, holding the two rings he'd purchased. "You'd better open it."

I poured the two rings into my hand, and said, "My dear Charles, they're wedding rings, aren't they?"

"Yes," he said, as he put one on my finger and the other on his. I didn't have the courage to spend the money when we married, but I've always thought we'd be married forever. I read somewhere that's what wedding rings stand for." Tears began to quietly run down his cheeks. "It looks like we'll have to say good-bye sooner than I thought, but I'll be waiting for you in heaven. And this time, dear woman, you won't have to live in a shanty."

I held on to Charles but could only squeeze out "I love you" through my tears. We knew the children would be needing us, so finished our work, gained our composure and went inside.

We said nothing about our conversation until we were in bed. When we prayed together, as we usually did, we asked for healing for Charles and strength for me, as well as thanking God for the years we'd had together. When we were done, Charles whispered, "Let's make these next ten years as happy as possible, my love. I don't know about you, but I plan to savor every day."

28

The Unthinkable

"The last enemy to be destroyed is death."

1 Corinthians 15:26

Esther came home for the summer, knowing she wouldn't go back to school until September, and once again she complained the house was overfilled with children. On the other hand, she had much to tell us about what she'd been learning, especially about nutrition. She was obsessed with healthful eating and encouraged Charles and me to plant a wider variety of vegetables for the family. For the first time, she took an interest in the garden, as she planted and tended spinach, green beans, kale, herbs and several new tomato varieties she'd started from seeds given to her by one of her instructors at school because they were famed for their health value. Charles was glad for her interest and help. He was also grateful that he felt decent, though he now needed a nap almost every afternoon.

June was a beautiful month for growing with mild weather and soft rains. The hay fields were lush, and our planted crops germinated well and were far ahead of usual years.

For the summer months Charles had decided to make his milk deliveries on Monday, Wednesday and Friday, so he could have the whole day home to work the fields on Tuesday, Thursday, and Saturday. Charles and I often spoke about how nice it would be when the boys would grow up and use some of their limitless energy to work rather than play.

After breakfast Charles kissed me good-bye and said he'd be in the north field for the morning, hilling potatoes. I watched him walk with his hoe to the field, pausing to pet the dog, and pick up a stray ball on his way.

I knew the potato patch could only be described as magnificent. The plants are dark green and bushy. Charles is probably the exceptional man, who truly enjoys working in his fields. He has told me it gives him time to think and to converse with God.

The day has turned warm, hot to be more precise, especially for June 21st. It is no doubt the warmest day of the year so far. As I wait for him to return from the fields, I hope Charles will take the children to the Stark swimming hole in the afternoon, so they can all cool off.

At noon, I send Herbert out to fetch his father for lunch. It irritates me that he is working so long in the hot sun. He'd told me he'd be in well before noon.

I hear Herbert's excited voice calling me, "Mother, Mother. Father's fallen. I ran towards Herbert, following him back to the field, where I can see a form that must be Charles lying on the ground.

When I reach him, I know instantly he is dead. I feel for a pulse, just to make sure, but find none. I remove my apron, covering him with it, thinking to protect him from the hot sun. I take Herbert's hand and walk with him back to the house. He asks question after question, but I make no attempt to answer them. Once inside, I ask for Esther's help to contact the pastor and the mortuary.

Esther looks at me as if I am insane. "Grown men don't just die. I'll examine him and see what's happened." She stomps out of the house, walking to the field, only to return with tears, announcing that Father is indeed dead. I ask her once again to walk to the service station and phone the mortician and the pastor, and this time she complies.

Within an hour after Esther returned, the mortician arrives. I did not understand how that happened so quickly, but I am thankful Charles' body has been removed from the hot sun. The mortician says he will contact the coroner, to determine a cause of death, since Charles looks healthy and was so young.

I hear the words, but don't comprehend them. In fact, the next week goes by in a blur for me. Somehow there is a lovely funeral at our little Lutheran Church. I recognize Charles' favorite hymns and scriptures and hear kind words spoken of him. I am pleased to see the church full of members and neighbors, and even some of Charles' milk customers, and the Gunderssons, but I am devastated to see him put to rest next to our son, Laurence.

Returning home is difficult. I catch myself looking for Charles wherever I go. I stay close to the children, having one on my lap or beside me at all times. Hulda and Nathalie take care of milking and feeding the animals. Someone (I don't remember who) suggests I sell the milk to Bridgeman's until the delivery route can be restarted, and that is arranged by Esther with the milk picked up each day and empty milk cans left off to refill.

Esther takes over the kitchen. The three little boys are put to work by her, but she soon realizes it takes more energy to guide them than to do the cooking herself. Reluctantly, she tells them to stay out of the kitchen, and they escape outside to play.

PART FIVE

Elina Heads the Soderberg Farm

She rises while it is yet night and provides food for her household and tasks for her maidens."

Proverbs 31:15

29

The Virtuous Woman

"Favour is deceitful, and beauty is vain; but a woman that feareth the LORD, she shall be praised."

Proverbs 31:30

I feel as if I am in an extended nightmare, but even in my confused state I know it will not end. I have lost four babies and somehow survived, so I tell myself I will survive now also. However, the truth is I have no desire to live. Then one evening at supper, almost a month after Charles has died, I look around the crowded table and realize I am responsible for the seven children sitting there. That evening I go to the barn and know I am no less responsible for the thirty cows, the four sheep, the thirty chickens and even the dog and cats. I remember, after Laurence died, Charles held me by my by my shoulders and told me that we could not afford the luxury of grieving. I know that once again I have to wake up and get to work even though I don't have the slightest desire to do so. I push myself to go on, and first I ask Esther where she's put the farm ledger. When she gets it for me, I sit at the table and recognize the last entry, on June 20, 1910, is the day before Charles had died. I realize no bills have been paid during the past weeks, nor has any of the milk income been recorded. Esther tells me that Bridgeman's pays for the milk twice a month, so there probably are payments in the pile of mail on top of the trunk.

 I take down the mail and sort it into bills, cards and letters, and unknown, which I call miscellaneous. I open the bills for ice, cow feed, chicken feed, and seeds, all things Charles normally paid for after his Wednesday milk deliveries. I total the bills and am relieved I have money to pay them on Monday. I am surprised to find many sympathy cards with many containing gifts of money. I know the mortician had left thank you cards, along with many other sympathy cards and decide the girls and I should write thank you notes on Sunday. The miscellaneous stack contains an alarmingly large bill from the mortician. I remember Charles expressing his surprise over bills from Laurence's funeral, but somehow he had taken care of them. Now it will be my job to pay the bill for Charles' funeral. I also find a milk check from Bridgeman's that I will use to pay a fraction of the funeral costs. Not willing to live blindly any more, I take the "money envelopes" out of their hiding place and count what is in each envelope. I remember the household expense envelope is in my sewing basket, where I could access it easily and find $14.57 in it. I count and write the contents on each of the other envelopes: farm expenses: $32.72; emergencies: $62.00; new house fund: $1609. I am surprised to find an envelope that Charles had added: school fund for children in which there was already $87.00 written on the envelope. I pray about the expenses and come to two decisions. I will need to use much of the new house fund to pay the mortician's fees and though the selling of milk to Bridgeman's has been extremely convenient, it cut our milk income almost by half by not selling directly to customers, and we cannot go on earning so little. I take out Charles' box of customer cards with deliveries written on them and find there is even money due from many customers. It is not what I want to do, but realize I have no choice but to take over deliveries and decide to start in August while Esther is still home from school. I also know I will need to hire men to help with haying. There is no way to do that by myself or even with the help of the girls. I will walk over to the Aaron Stark farm in the morning and ask for suggestions of someone to hire. With a plan in mind, I go to bed, and instead of lying wide awake for hours, as I'd been doing for many nights, I fall asleep immediately after praying.

Morning comes quickly, but I get up and add more things to my "to do" list, realizing I have to tell my father about Charles' death, and that I have to look over the garden carefully to prioritize what needs to be done. I go to the barn to check on Hulda and Nathalie, asking them if they needed anything. They seem sad, and I hug them both, telling them how much I appreciate the work they've been doing. Hulda whispers, "I miss my father" and when all three of us start to cry, we can only hold each other and share our grief.

I check the milk house and see that the ice is dangerously low, so immediately after breakfast tell Esther where I am going, and after hitching the horses to the wagon, drive the short distance to the gas station at the corner that has ice for sale. With enough ice on the wagon to last until Monday afternoon, for the first time I pay for something, using money from Charles' money pouch. I ask for a receipt, so I will be sure to enter the correct amount in the farm ledger, and then travel to the Aaron Stark farm to get some advice about help for haying. Aaron invites me into their cozy kitchen, where his wife, Ida, is feeding six month old Alfhild. The couple extend their condolences and ask how they can help. I immediately ask about who I can hire for haying, and Mr. Stark surprises me by saying he'd send a couple of fellows my way the following Monday, if it isn't raining. I am relieved by his helpfulness, and when I ask how much I should pay them, he suggests two dollars per day per man. I thank him, refuse Ida's offer of coffee, and hurry home to unload the ice in the milk house.

I spend much of the day answering Esther's questions. She is concerned she will not be able to go back to St. Luke's School of Nursing, but I assure her she will be able to do so. As I answer her, I wonder how I'll even be able to function in the fall with Esther gone and Nathalie, Harry and Victor in school. I will have to take Herbert and Ruth with me on deliveries. They will have to play in a basket on the wagon. Somehow, with God's help, it will work. Nathalie and Hulda seem more than willing to continue with the milking if I am able to do the separating and bottling. That only seems fair, but then I have to ask Nathalie if she'd be able to take over bread making in the fall, and she answers, "I would love to do that."

Sunday, we go to church for the first time without Charles. It is difficult for me, but I make it through the service and appreciate the kind words of the congregation. That afternoon, Esther, Nathalie and I write out thank you notes for sympathy gifts.

When my "to do" list is written out for the next day I start the job I'd been dreading, that of writing to my father:

July 20, 1910
My dear Father:

Just when I thought nothing worse could happen, Charles has died. On June 21, almost a month ago, we had breakfast together, and he commented on what a beautiful day it was. He went out to the fields to hill potatoes and died right in the field.

Here I am 41 years old and a widow. I have lost three little girls and buried one son, and now I am left with seven children I must somehow support. Esther is 18 and won't be much help as she will continue nurses' training in the fall. Hulda, at 15, is good-hearted, but very distractible. She happily spends most of her days with the animals. Nathalie is my best help, but she is only 12, and I fear I've already cheated her of too much of her childhood. The boys are growing strong and bright, but they're young. Harry is 9, Victor 7, and Herbert is 4. And then there's little Ruth who is only 3., Charles and I have taken care of the farm together, but at the moment I feel weak and unfit to run the farm by myself. The house we've planned to build is now simply a far-fetched dream. I will work hard to feed the family and somehow send them to school. I am thankful you taught me the importance of education. It was very important to Charles also.

I reread what I have written, crumple it up and throw it in the fire. It was full of the self-pity that I feel, but cannot and will not allow myself to wallow in. Actually after writing how I felt, I am able to put some of my negative feelings aside—at least temporarily. I rewrite the letter, simply and factually, ending by writing "with the help of God the children and I will not only survive but eventually thrive."

I decide I will use the rest of July to prepare the children for what they'll need to do, before starting deliveries. That will give me a month to figure out the route, and then when school starts, I would take Herbert and Ruth with me.

Mr. Stark has referred two hired men to me to do the haying, but their help can't go beyond haying season, especially with our income being cut so drastically. I began jotting down notes in a notebook, realizing I can bring the beans, spinach, beets and lettuce with me to sell. Corn and tomatoes and potatoes will be ready later. The crops look beautiful, and I wonder whether Harry and Victor would want to sell produce at a stand right on the road. They could earn some money and stay out of mischief. Gradually, I have a trickle of hope. That evening I thank God for the hope, and almost immediately after my head hits the pillow, I fall into a peaceful sleep, waking refreshed and ready to take over the milk delivery.

But first things first: milking the cows, eating breakfast, and then a family meeting. I settle Ruth and Herbert on the floor with toys, and then I say I need to talk with the rest of them. I start with a prayer, thanking God for his goodness, and asking Him for guidance. And then, as the children's eyes grew big, I talk about how much I miss their father and know they do also, but I also know he would want all of us to work together on the farm he loved so much. I told them that I believe that God has been leading me into a plan, and I want them to think about what they can do to help: "Esther, we know you'll be going back to St. Luke's Nursing School in the fall, but will you be able to keep on with the kitchen work until then?"

"Yes, Mother, I can, but you know I can't get the hang of bread making."

"That's all right. I know it's a problem for you, and I've already asked Nathalie to help with bread. Hulda, I'm going to ask you to stay home this year to help in the barn, but you tell me after that when you want to go to agriculture school."

"That's good," said Hulda, sounding relieved she did not have to go to school right away.

"Nathalie, when Esther leaves, I'd like your help in the kitchen, but I'd like you to take over bread making right away. I'm ready to take over barn work with Hulda, so don't think I expect you to do everything."

Dear Nathalie replied, "I can keep helping in the barn till school starts, and I'd love to bake the bread."

"Harry and Victor, I'm going to start teaching you how to do more jobs. You'll have time to play, but you two are now the men in the house, and I need your help."

Harry and Victor look at each other and almost start to laugh, but I look at them so sternly, they both nod with not the hint of a smile.

"I know I have to start the milk deliveries next month, and I'll be leaving Esther in charge. We have next week to practice. When school starts, I'll take Herbert and Ruth with me, but for now I'll leave them at home for all of you to take turns watching. And I forgot one thing. Our vegetable garden is beautiful though greatly in need of weeding, which you boys can start today. I'd like to take produce with me on the milk route, and I think we should also have a stand right by the gas station until school starts. I'll check with Mr. Erickson today to see if he'll let us have a stand close to his business. That way his customers might shop after completing their business with him. And Harry and Victor, how about you manning the stand, selling the vegetables? You're both good at counting money, and I think you might be able to earn some of your own.

Hulda spoke up, "I don't want to sell vegetables, but I'd like to earn some money."

"That seems fair, Hulda. Let me think of a way that will work for all of you. Now is there anything else?"

Esther asks the question I've wanted to avoid: "Will the building of the house start this fall?"

"No, Esther, and truthfully I don't know whether we will be able to build a house. Now, it's much more important that I'm able to save money, so all of you can go to school to be prepared for a career. Now, everyone tell me what their job is today?"

The children all answer. Harry and Victor have already forgotten about weeding, but I will teach them that necessary skill. They'll start with the potatoes and corn, where it is easiest to tell the weeds apart from the vegetables.

Everyone gets busy with their jobs, and I take my two eager boys to the potato patch. I bring a hoe with but realize immediately it is way too long for Harry and Victor. I show them the potato plants, pointing out the characteristic wrinkled leaves and dark green color. As they walk up the row, the boys spot weeds, and I show them how important it is to pull them out by the roots. That is more difficult for the boys, so I have Harry run to the storage shed to get two small spades. When he returns, with boy-sized tools, they experience success. I assign the boys the job of finishing the whole potato field by Saturday night. They think they can easily get it done, though I'm not as confident. Before I leave the field, I hill half a row of potatoes, starting at the spot where Charles must have been stopped. Instead of thinking about it too long, I quickly hill the remaining row and go to the milk house to help Hulda and Nathalie process the milk.

30

The Seller of Merchandise

"She perceiveth that her merchandise is good: her candle goeth not out by night."

Proverbs 31:18

The very next Monday I began making milk deliveries. With the milk that had accumulated the previous week, I make cheese and butter, which I will also sell along with bushel baskets of beans, lettuce, spinach, and beets.

With Charles' customer cards in a box beside me, I drive onto the Stark Road directly into Proctor. I make my first stop, knocking on the door, and asking if the woman who answered wantsany milk.

She answers, "I buy from Mr. Soderberg, but he hasn't stopped by for weeks."

"I'm Elina Soderberg. My husband died last month, and now I'll be delivering on Mondays, Wednesdays, and Fridays."

"I'm sorry. I didn't know he'd died. Let me get the empties for you, and I'll meet you at your wagon."

She takes two quarts of milk, a pound of butter, and after tasting a sample, a pound of cheese. Then she adds beans, spinach and beets.

I am good at adding in my head and tell her she owes four dollars and fifty cents. She pays me, thanks me, and says she'd like me to stop Monday, Wednesday, and Friday. I jot down the days I should stop and how much the woman paid before driving to my next stop, where I repeat the same routine.

Most stops are very easy with friendly, honest customers. A few are more difficult. For example, there was a debt of six dollars written on the customer card for one family, but the man who answered the door said I was wrong. What could I say? For all I knew it was a mistake—though I doubted it. He pays for his purchases and asks me to stop on Wednesday and Friday also. This time I write "cash only" on his customer card.

And that's how the morning goes. I have 25 stops to make in Proctor and 52 in West Duluth. I am back at home by one, without making any of the extra stops I'd planned. I am not discouraged, however, because it was my first delivery route, and I needed to introduce myself to each customer and determine whether they want to continue milk delivery. I also realize that Monday will be my busiest day followed by Friday. About one-fourth of my customers do not request Wednesday deliveries, so that will be my day for errands.

The children had done fine at home while I was gone. I had long since realized that Esther was not only a capable task master but enjoyed being in charge of her siblings. No one seemed unhappy, and I am pleased to notice there had been significant weeding done in the gardens. I thought I would continue with the weeding, but after eating a bit, I am tired and fall sound asleep while reading the mail. I understand, now, why an afternoon nap was very important to Charles. Nevertheless, when I get up I began supper, noting that Nathalie had baked rye bread while I was gone. I smile when I see the beautiful round loaves and then begin cooking new potatoes I will add to left over fish to make a quick stew.

31

Clothing for Children

"She is not afraid of snow for her household, for all her household are clothed in scarlet."

Proverbs 31:21

I have little time for anything but work, but I cannot complain. The milk route goes better each day, and I enjoy the brief visits with my customers. They are eager to purchase my products, which makes the experience a pleasure.

I know that the children need clothing, and one Wednesday bring all the children but Esther and Hulda with me to shop after my abbreviated deliveries. The customers seem impressed by the children, and the children are patient and sociable at each stop.

We stop at a clothing store in West Duluth where I am shocked by the price of a new pair of shoes for five children, pants and shirts for three boys and skirts and blouses for two girls. I add socks and underwear and know my income for the day is almost used up, and that doesn't take into account a shopping trip Esther and Hulda will take on their own. It is the first summer I had not spent time sewing school clothes, but I know for this year I had made a practical decision. Before I head home, we stop at a second hand clothing store where I find thee warm coats in good condition. Those, along with outgrown jackets Amanda has given me will assure the children will be warm when winter arrives.

Esther leaves for St. Luke's School of Nursing at the end of August. She rides on the milk wagon with Herbert, Ruth and me. She has a satchel with her, along with her money for tuition and board, and extra dollars for spending money I gave her to say thank you for all of her work over the summer. She is excited to return to school, but takes the time to hug her siblings and me before climbing aboard a streetcar.

As school starts for Nathalie, Harry and Victor, I am thankful that Hulda will be at home for another year. She doesn't talk much about agriculture school, except to say she's heard St. Paul is a big city, but I am determined she will have the opportunity to go eventually.

I begin taking Herbert and Ruth on the milk route, and they enjoy going with me and meeting many of my customers, who dote on the children and often treat them to a cookie or apple. I am concerned what will happen when the weather turns cold and pray for a solution so am very thankful, but not surprised, when one of my Proctor customers asks me if I would consider leaving Herbert and Ruth with her during my deliveries in exchange for milk. I know the woman has little money and that the children will be happy with her, so it is an easy offer to accept. With that solution in place, life instantly becomes less difficult. Not easy, however, as I still rise every morning at 4:30, milk the cows with Hulda, process the milk and load it on the wagon while Nathalie makes breakfast and often starts bread. I eat with the children, making sure they are clean and set for their day and pray with them all before we get on the wagon to which Hulda has hitched the horses that are in her care. I drop off Nathalie, Harry and Victor at the schoolhouse and continue on my way with Herbert and Ruth to Proctor. With deliveries done, including the delivery of Herbert and Ruth, I go on to my West Duluth deliveries, run whatever errands I need to do and return home after picking up Herbert and Ruth.

Once home, I turn over the horses and wagon to Hulda, while I make a quick lunch for the four of us. I insist that Herbert, who has long ago given up naps, remains quiet for an hour while Ruth rests and usually I do also.

It was during one of these quiet times that I hear a knock on the door. When I look out the window I recognize the man to whom I'd seen Charles frequently giving money. I almost don't open the door, but it is raining, and I feel pity for him.

As he comes in out of the rain, I say, "Sir, I know my husband gave you money, but he died in July, and I have no money to give you."

"I know Charles died, and I'm sorry for your loss, Mrs. Soderberg. I feel I knew your huband well, and I know he was a fine man. I'm not here for money. In fact, I have money to give to you."

"I don't understand."

"Your husband took out a life insurance policy to provide for you and your children if something were to happen to him, and if you will provide me with a death certificate, I will give you the check."

I had been given three death certificates, and at the time I hadn't known why I would need any of them, but, nevertheless, I had carefully put them away and now retrieved one from my chest of drawers to give to the man who had introduced himself as Mr. Johnson.

In exchange, he handed me a check from Aid Association for Lutherans made out to me for fifteen thousand dollars. I look at him incredulously. "Please explain this to me," is all I can manage to say.

He patiently explains to me how life insurance works, emphasizing how much of a help it is to widows like myself.

"Sir, this is a miracle to me. I've prayed steadily that I would be able to meet the needs of my children, and here is the answer to my prayers. Thank you."

"It is your husband who should have been thanked, not me, but you can thank God for leading him to buy insurance. We started our company in 1902 in Wisconsin, and Charles was one of my first clients in Minnesota."

After giving me suggestions for how to use the money, the man from AAL leaves. I am overwhelmed with appreciation for Charles' wisdom and foresight. No wonder, he'd felt so confident we would build a house—even after learning he was ill. The next day, after delivering milk, I bring the check to a bank. Mr. Johnson had told me would need to bring a death certificate with me, which I did, in order to cash the check. The banker discourages me greatly from taking so much cash with me, but I have no trust in banks and insist on my stubborn desire. Finally he agrees, telling me to deposit it in whatever bank I wish as, soon as possible.

After picking up Herbert and Ruth I drive home with thoughts spinning in my mind. After the children have lunch and are settled for rests, I enter my sales and the bills I'd paid in my ledger book. I also made an entry of $15,000 from life insurance under income. Accustomed to writing a few dollars and cents, I check three times to make certain I have entered the sum correctly. I then take my savings envelopes from their safe place in the locked wooden box. Since paying for Charles' funeral service and for the two men who had done the haying for me, the envelopes have remained nearly empty with the exception of the 10 per cent I faithfully place in my tithing envelope, the few dollars I set aside each week for our daily expenses, and the thirty dollars Charles had somehow managed to accumulate for Hulda's schooling. With great joy I take out the $1500 for tithing, and then put one hundred dollars for each of the children, in the education envelope. I am thrilled to know there will be no worry about paying for Esther's third year of nurses' training. I then put $1,000 in the envelope for emergencies, and $500 each in the family expenses and farm expenses envelopes. When I count what is left over, I know that the $10,800 is more than enough for the house Charles and I had planned. I hide the envelopes away in a gap between the boards in my bedroom floor. As I come out of my room, the door opens and Nathalie, Victor and Harry rush in. As I pour them glasses of milk and give them slices of bread and butter for a snack, the sun unexpectedly breaks through the clouds. I smile broadly at my beautiful children and take time to hug each and of them and tell them I love them. It is a day I will never forget, I think to myself, as I gaze at my family.

32

The Years Pass

"But you are not in the flesh, you are in the Spirit, if the Spirit of God really dwells in you. Any one who does not have the spirit of Christ does not belong to him. But if Christ is in you, although your bodies are dead because of sin, your spirits are alive because of righteousness. If the Spirit of him who raised Jesus from the dead dwells in you, he who raised Christ Jesus from the dead will give life to your mortal bodies also through his Spirit which dwells in you."

Romans 8:9-11

The next fall, 1911, Herbert starts school, and Ruth, who has never been separated from her brother, is heartbroken. At age four she is determined she should join him, and consequently spends her days teaching herself to read and write. Any paper that Herbert brings home is claimed by Ruth. She then first asks Herbert and then Nathalie "to teach it" to her. By the time she starts school in the fall of 1912, she is not only well ahead of her classmates but is determined to become a teacher.

Esther starts her third year of nurses' training, looking forward to graduating and starting her nursing career. She is studying to become a public nurse and is passionate about wanting to work in Duluth with young mothers and their children.

Hulda promises me she will go to Ag School whenever Nathalie will go with her. She did not, under any conditions, want to go to a big school by herself. Harry, 10, and Victor, 8, continue to attend the Midway School while Nathalie is attending high school in Proctor.

I receive a letter from my sister Josefina, telling me my father has died. It is not a surprise since he was 87 years old, but it saddens me that he never saw his grandchildren.

I am proud of how our family is growing up and realize we really do not fit in our tiny house. I try to hire a builder to start our house in 1914, only to be met with his refusal due to the war. He is certain the United States will enter the war, and he intends to enlist. I am disappointed by his refusal but much more disturbed by the possibility of the United States' entrance into a war. For the first time, I subscribe to an English newspaper, so we can learn what is happening in the world. Unfortunately, I learn of much tragedy and unrest not only on a world level but even in Duluth.

When the United States enters the War in 1917 I pray fervently that peace will come and that my boys will not have to serve. God answers my prayers for my sons as well as for our builder, who is found physically unfit for military service and therefore able to begin building our new home in 1917.

The carpenter's work goes surprisingly smoothly, and the house is more beautiful than I had ever imagined it would be. The front faces the Stark road and has a porch across it. Upon entering the front door there is a foyer with a door to the kitchen on the right, a door to the parlor on the left and a beautiful open stairway straight ahead leading to four bedrooms.

The family will use the back door most often, which goes through a spacious entryway into the generously-sized farm kitchen, where built-in cabinets run along one wall. Alongside the kitchen is a pantry, complete with shelves and a counter. As the building proceeds, I have the entire farm wired with electricity, and there is a water pump in both the kitchen and basement, bringing amazing conveniences. I have water and electricity brought to the barn and other outbuildings at the same time. Harry says, "Mother, you've brought the farm into the twentieth century. I did put my foot down with one item—an indoor bathroom. We have a large bathtub and means to heat water in the basement, but I cannot understand the appeal of indoor bathrooms. My children call me old-fashioned, but I cannot understand why a family would want to defile their own home by relieving themselves in it when they could do so in an outhouse, keeping odors and germs outside.

Past the pantry is the dining room with a beautiful built-in china cabinet including glassed shelves and deep drawers. A small room is directly off the dining room, and the builder has suggested it be an office or a sewing room, but I believe it will make a good room for me when I can no longer walk up the steps.

Half walls of glassed shelves separate the dining room from the parlor. Both rooms have large windows looking out onto the lawn in the front and the barn and outbuildings in the back. Oak has been used throughout the house, with the woodwork stained dark and the floors remaining natural. With the many windows the house feels light and airy. Nevertheless, I choose white or off-white for the paint except where I use touches of green and yelow in the kitchen.

With the new house only about thirty yards from the old one, moving will be very simple, but I feel I should furnish the new house with new furniture before we move in. The time for crate-made shelves and tables has come to an end. Planning carefully for the furniture expenses, I bring home furniture on the milk wagon most days for two weeks. I choose four large brass beds and mattresses, eight chests of drawers for the bedrooms and an armoire for the upstairs hall. I also choose two large round tables, one in dark oak with matching chairs for the dining room and one in lighter oak for the kitchen. Both have leaves to make the tables extra large.

I choose a sofa and two chairs for the parlor along with lamps, a small bed and chest of drawers for the extra bedroom, along with several electric lamps, and then, with the house minimally but well-furnished, I temporarily run out of money. We move kitchen chairs and the large immigrant trunk into the new house and hang up the picture of my Swedish home, Ljungsjömåla, our wedding picture, and the citizenship certificate of which Charles was so proud. We each take a load of kitchen items and a load of clothing into the new house, and the move is complete.

We eat our first meal in the new kitchen, elated with our new surroundings. I had butchered two chickens, which Nathalie has fried along with sweet parsnips from the garden. Esther has made a big garden salad of lettuce, cucumbers, tomatoes and onions and cooked corn on the cob.

Ruth, now 10 years old, says, "This is truly a feast!" The rest of the family is in agreement.

The last task I do that night is to unpack my trunk. I use the sheets I'd embroidered to make up the beds for the girls. I unpack doilies and dresser scarves I hadn't looked at in 20 years and find just the right spot for each.

I even put the handkerchief I'd embroidered and my kidskin gloves into my chest of drawers and hang my fancy dresses in my closet, knowing they had come from a different era —and a different life. I look at my strong, calloused hands and know they aren't even close to fitting into my kid gloves. I think of the cows I've milked, the children I've held, and the husband I've caressed with them and weep not at my increased hand size but with gratitude for the great service they've given me and my family. At the same time I feel the great loneliness I have in my heart, the deep sadness for my lost children and especially for Charles but once again manage to thank our heavenly Father for the joy of having had Charles as my husband for 22 years and for the gift of children. Now I will go on, as best I can, in a house Charles would have been proud to own.

33

Fire

"As with the rumbling of chariots, they leap on the tops of the mountains like the crackling of a flame of fire..."

Joel 2:5

The summer of 1918 is unusually dry and hot. The necessity of frequent watering is added to the long list of farm chores. I am thankful that Harry, Victor and Herbert are strong boys. They haul pails of water to the fields for hours each day with the result of surprisingly good production. Herbert and Ruth now man the vegetable stand on the corner of Midway and Stark Roads, and each year the money earned through this endeavor has increased. While in ag school, Victor had learned about a two-colored variety of corn that is especially sweet. He persuaded me to let him plant it, and now we are reaping the rewards. Customers who taste it came back repeatedly.

Harry will return to the University of Minnesota in the fall, but for the summer not only is he helping on the farm, but he is working as a bicycle messenger in West Duluth. Because he works some nights and then sleeps days, he lives in our little house where he is not bothered by the commotion of our large family.

In October, the biggest squash and pumpkins we've ever grown are ripening. The days are miserable, however, due to strong, hot winds that not only cause sand and soil to hit people and animals, but are downright eerie. On the eleventh of October, the sun never breaks through the clouds of dark smoke that surround the farm. Harry rides his bicycle home at noon to tell us that there are small fires all around, especially along the railroad tracks. Since a track cuts diagonally through one of our fields, instead of using the buckets to water crops that day, we soak down the grass on the west side of the tracks. I tell the children to pray our family and neighbors will be safe. Hulda asks about the animals, and I tell her to pray for them also.

I run from the outside pump with buckets of water that I start pouring around the house. The water seems to evaporate before it even hits the ground, but I truly don't know what else to do. The thought of losing our home sickens me, but I know the outcome of fire is in God's hands and ask only for protection of my children.

That night we all go to bed, exhausted from working in the wind. The next morning we wake to the same smoky conditions, but now even the animals are extremely nervous. Our dog, Star, howls hour on end. The animals are obviously sensing fire, and as a family we continue to pour water on the western edge of the tracks and around the house and barn. Harry has gone to work during the night but returns by noon, telling us fires are on their way. By two o'clock the wind picks up, and it is difficult to even stand up outside. I kept the cows and chickens in the barn, believing in their agitated state, they would run away.

Unable to complete any farm work but milking, I tell the children we should all stay in the basement. We bring Charles' and our wedding picture, Charles' Citizenship Declaration and the picture of Ljungsjömåla into the basement along with apples and cheese and even a few blankets. I run back up the stairs to claim the ledger book and the beautiful wooden bird Charles carved for me so many years ago. The electricity soon goes out, so we can't even see each other. With no car we decide to simply stay in the basement, putting our safety in the hands of God. We listen to the winds howl and feel heat creep down the stairs, but never spot fire on our land. Finally, about seven in the evening, Star runs up the stairs, followed by Mittens, demanding to go outside. We follow right behind, trusting the instinct of our pets.

The air is still, and dense smoke hangs everywhere. Harry starts on his way to Duluth to work his twelve hour night shift as a bicycle messenger, but returns soon to report what has happened. The fire had gone through, burning everything in its path. It had been approximately a mile away from us, but our family and farm have been preserved by God's mercy.

Throughout the next day, several men visit us on horseback, making sure we are all right and reporting on losses: Our neighbor, Emil Helmer's, farm has burned to the ground. The blacksmith's place, Holombo's, less than a mile from our farm, had been razed. The Mattson's home, which is straight west of Aaron Stark's farm has been destroyed. All of the buildings in the Adolph area, including the home of my sister, Amanda burned. Fortunately, Amanda, August and their children escaped in August's automobile. All of Scanlon and the city of Cloquet have been destroyed along with much of Esko, Moose Lake, Kettle River, Brookston and Moose Lake. Little damage has been done in Duluth, where thousands of people from the surrounding areas are being treated for burns and smoke inhalation. In Proctor the fire was mostly contained in the railroad roundhouse.

The fire did not touch our farm, but it did jump the river to the east side. Some people said it looked just as if the air were burning. Someone described their home as the fire hit, as if it exploded.

On Sunday, we attended a somber service at church. Pleas were made to help people who had lost their homes, and besides donating from our ample food supply, I offer our old home to Amanda, who declines my offer. The Mattsons, however, gratefully accept, and gratefully move in the same day.

34

Time Goes By

"For everything there is a season, and a time for every matter under heaven: a time to be born, and a time to die; a time to plant, and a time to pluck up what is planted; a time to kill and a time to heal; a time to break down and a time to build up; a time to weep and a time to laugh; a time to mourn and a time to dance; a time to cast away stones and a time to gather stones together; a time to embrace and a time to refrain from embracing; a time to seek and a time to lose; a time to keep and a time to cast away; a time to rend and a time to sew; a time to keep silence and a time to speak; a time for war and a time for peace."

Ecclesiastes 3:1-8

It seems to me that time has passed more quickly since our new house has been built. Perhaps it is the fact that we aren't waiting for it to be completed, or more probably it is the age of the children, as their personalities and dreams are clarified, or closest to the truth, I have grown old.

The same year our house had been built, the new Evangelical Church of Midway had also been built. Under the leadership of Pastor Christian Swenson, its name had been changed to the Augustana Lutheran Church of Midway. I feel deep satisfaction that all but Herbert and Ruth have already been confirmed in their faith. The family take turns reading the Bible at supper and join in family prayers. That is especially important to me because since Charles died, my attendance at church services has been very poor. I would like to attend, but I can't find the hours on Sunday morning, and the few times I have gone, I have embarrassed myself by falling asleep during the service. I have asked for our pastor's forgiveness, and he told me not to worry about attending services until the boys can take over more of the work on the farm. His kind words freed me of much guilt. He knows that I read the Bible and pray often and make sure the children go to church, Sunday School and confirmation. He smiles and says, "With the size of your family you have your own congregation at home. He does give Hulda, who is too introverted to attend church, and me communion whenever he comes to visit, and I am thankful for that.

In 1919, to the country's relief, World War I ends. I celebrate my fiftieth birthday, and realize I am getting old though anyone watching me work on the farm would have doubted it as I run from one task to another. Esther is 27 years old but hasn't seemed able or willing to settle down into her career. She has finished her nurses' training as a public health nurse, and then after working a short time, decided to take a business course at the University of Minnesota. Instead of coming home when it was done, she continued with Bible courses. After that, she worked for a few years at a series of temporary positions, and now she is home, performing minimal work on the farm and reading during every spare minurte. I've attempted to ask her about her plans but have been met with unreasonable anger. I know Charles would have known how to talk with her, but I feel I need to give her time to decide how to apply her abilities.

Hulda, now 24, is content to work on the farm. She and Nathalie went to Ag School together, after Nathalie had completed a year of high school. They spent six months there, completing two quarters of work. I know Nathalie would have stayed longer, but when Hulda had had enough, Nathalie, ever the good sister, accompanied her home. She spoke of the wonderful training she'd received in cooking and baking and, at 19, has completely taken over our farm kitchen, doing a much better job than I've ever done. I know Nathalie has several young men interested in courting her and suspect she will marry soon.

Harry graduated from Proctor High School and enrolled at the University of Minnesota. He is a scholar, who loves school and does extremely well. I think he will probably end up teaching and doubt he will ever return to the farm except to visit.

Victor completed one year of high school and then went to the Ag School, graduating after two years. He came home, very interested in farming and told me he would like to raise chickens, lots of them. He asked if he could work at the home farm until he marries. He's taken over the delivery of milk. With the money I pay him, he has bought forty acres of land on the Midway Road, for his own farm, within a mile of ours.

With all of the changes, I'm glad I'll have Herbert at 13 and Ruth at 12 home with me for a while longer.

During the summer of 1922, Hulda has a spell of sickness that I can't understand. Usually docile and quiet, she has become argumentative and even physically aggressive. She refuses to do any work and spends her days and nights in the barn, and much to my concern, she has become very demanding of Nathalie, insisting she take care of her to the point that she wants to be read to and to be fed.

Not knowing what else to do, I contact Dr. Monson, asking him to make a house call. Telling me he no longer makes house calls, he agrees to send his associate, who comes on October 22, the third day during which Hulda has refused to even speak. The doctor tells me he wants one more person to examine her and will admit her to the hospital until it is done. It is a relief to me as I watch her ride away in his car to Duluth. What I don't realize he will do is bring her before a judge, who declares her insane. Within a few days, on October 26, she is admitted to the Fergus Falls Hospital for the Insane with a diagnosis of dementia praecox. I don't believe the doctor attempted to trick me into hospitalizing

Hulda. He no doubt informed me of exactly what he was doing, but somehow I was too overwhelmed by Hulda's behavior to understand what was happening.

And if I had understood, I don't even know what I would have done. I knew something was terribly wrong with Hulda and that none of us at the farm could help her or even handle her. But was she mentally ill? I don't think so. I know Hulda is stubborn and probably the least bright of my children, but that certainly doesn't mean she is insane. The word is simply too harsh and too cruel and too incorrect.

Each week I phone the hospital in Fergus Falls from the corner gas station and ask about Hulda. I am told she is adjusting well, and that after a month she can have visitors. I think the month will never end, but it finally does, and nineteen-year-old Victor drives me the two hundred miles to the hospital in the Model T I'd finally purchased to use for milk deliveries. When I first see the hospital it reminds me of a Swedish castle, but when we enter, all comparisons end. There is no luxury and little beauty inside the building that is over one-third of a mile long. The first floor has a large waiting area and halls of offices. People are milling around, more like insects than humans.

Once we have been seen by a "family intake expert" Hulda is brought to us. To my joy, she is clean, calm and talkative. There is an attendant with her at all times, but I see no signs of the unrest she'd displayed at home. She shows us "where she lives," actually a cot with a bedside table in an endless row. She gives us a brief tour of the 500 acre farm on which the asylum is located. It is a beautiful setting, and Hulda is excited to show us the healthy animals.

Victor and I are led back to the "intake center" where a doctor is finally able to talk with us. He tells us Hulda has adjusted well to her care. In fact, he says she's become highly cooperative. He also tells me testing has identified her as feeble-minded, meaning she cannot learn as well as most people. That is no surprise to me since she had struggled so much at school, but the label is still terrible. I ask when he thinks she will be able to return home, and he indicates the hospital staff prefers to keep the legally insane for a minimum of a year to make certain they are stable.

Victor asks what kind of treatment Hulda is receiving. The doctor explains that the overall treatment is healthy food and hygiene, lots of sunshine and fresh air, a clearly defined routine, and opportunities to work on the farm.

He asks if she is receiving medicine, and the doctor replies, "There is no medicine to treat insanity."

"Then she's not really receiving anything that we couldn't supply to her in her own home," I tentatively say.

"I have no idea what you can supply at your home. I only know it was at your home where she became mentally ill."

"The reply is like a slap on my face. His clear implication is that something at home has caused her illness. Victor must have recognized my discomfort, as he says we would like to say good-bye to Hulda, and then we will leave. From somewhere an attendant brings Hulda to us. We exchange farewells, and I ask Hulda if she would like us to come again. She answers that would be "fine," and seems unconcerned that we are leaving.

Victor drives back to the farm. I want to talk with him about our visit, but the noise from the car is way too loud. Give me a horse-drawn buggy anytime! When we arrive home, Victor kindly says, "When you want to visit Hulda again, just let me know, and I'll drive you."

"But it wasn't a very satisfactory visit."

"You're correct, Mother, but imagining how she's doing would be even less satisfactory."

We go to visit her close to Christmas and again in March for her birthday, along with a few times in the summer. She seems fine to both of us, and finally the hospital staff agrees with us and releases her in February of 1924. My arthritis was acting up at the time, so Nathalie offers to take the train to Fergus Falls to accompany Hulda back.

Hulda is happy to be home, especially to see Socks and Mittens, her cats. The following day, she wakes up early and begins milking cows. She is shocked to find I've hire two farmhands, Oscar Elpseth, a young man in the neighborhood and Ernest Nelson, a Swedish citizen who lives with us about half of each year. He is in his mid-thirties and obviously interested in courting Nathalie. When I ask her about him, she says he is a very nice man, but she will never move to Sweden. She would not consider "leaving the family".

While Hulda had been hospitalized, Esther had not visited her but had done much research about mental illness. She would often walk into Proctor or ride with Victor and take a streetcar to the wonderful Duluth Public Library, spending the day in the medical section. She was not impressed with the care Victor and I reported Hulda was receiving and told us that mental illness is an "unexplored medical frontier." She told us many researchers believed it was caused by heredity not by environment. She talks about the "nurture versus nature" theory, something I don't truly understand, but seems to be Esther's latest obsession. For a while she talks of demon possession, as the source of her illness as described in the Bible. She expresses her insights to anyone who will listen to her.

However, when Hulda returns to us in 1924, Esther is impressed by how much healthier she appears to be. Esther is forever asking her questions about how she feels and about her care.

Five years later, in July of 1929, Esther rides with Victor into Duluth, supposedly to spend the day at the library, but she does not return that evening as expected. Instead we receive her phone message from a neighbor, telling us she is in the Fergus Falls Hospital, where she has voluntarily committed herself to the same hospital where Hulda had spent almost two years. Her actions are a complete mystery to me. Why would she choose to enter the hospital, especially the same hospital of which she was very critical while Hulda was there. I, of course, know she couldn't settle down into a career, even with the great deal of education at which she'd excelled, but that certainly didn't seem to be a reason to think she was insane.

I ask each of the children privately whether Esther had talked to them about her plans. Hulda has the most insight, saying "Esther told me there was something wrong with her, that she felt out of control. She didn't know how she could feel very sad and then very restless all in a short time. She did not want to be a burden to our family, and thought going to the hospital gave her a chance to get well like I did."

We corresponded with her by letter, visited her every other month and prayed for her. In May of 1931, she wrote telling us she was ready to come home. Victor traveled to Fergus Falls once again on May 22, signing her out into his care with the understanding she could return if she needed to do so.

I had not felt she was ill when she left, but upon her return it appeared her symptoms had intensified. The mood swings were very obvious, and whenever she got an idea, she would obsess on it. Mostly, she wanted to talk about salvation. We all believed in witnessing about our faith, but Esther did it in such a way that seemed somewhat threatening. If someone visited, even a small child, Esther would block their way out and ask them "If they'd been saved." She'd brought many people to tears, much to my concern. I knew Charles would have known how to deal with her, but I could only love her and pray for her.

Had I caused her disease? If so, I don't know how. She had been a happy, healthy child. She had a good mind and excelled in school. Growing up, she had had work to do on the farm, but all of the children did. I know of no traumatic events in her life. I seek for answers, reading the Bible and talking with our pastor, but I find none. I check out books at the library and read many theories I don't understand. I read about an Austrian, Sigmund Freud, who has developed something called psychoanalysis, but I don't want to take Esther to Austria. I try to talk with friends and acquaintances about mental illness but am confronted by a defensive wall. In the end, since no one is willing or able to discuss it, I turn to prayer, asking God to guide me and to take care of Esther. I sometimes worry what will happen to her after I die, but Victor assures me that not only will I live to an old age, but that he will look out for his sisters, including Esther. With that, I must let it rest.

35

New Families

"I am reminded of your sincere faith, a faith that dwelt first in your grandmother...."

2 Timothy 1:5

Time has gone by so fast. I never believed I would grow old so quickly, but now it is December, 1935, and I am 67 years old. My body is arthritic, and I do not have the energy nor the will to continue working as hard as I have for the last forty-five years, and thanks to my boys, Victor and Herbert, and dear Nathalie and Hulda, I don't need to do so. At Victor's request, I continue to keep the ledger book for the farm and pay the bills. I have learned to use a checkbook rather than deal with cash, but I must admit I miss Charles' envelope system.

I find I spend much time remembering both the happy and sad times of our lives. I make frequent visits to the cemetery, thinking of my babies and especially Charles. I would so like to talk with him. I hope that somehow he knows that I finally am beginning to grasp the many ideas he tried to teach me.

He spoke often of how costly love is. I grasped the idea that for everyone we love, we would have the pain of disappointment and loss. With every relationship, parent and child, lovers, friends, there will come a time of separation—by one person growing out of the relationship, by moving away, or by death. What I want to tell Charles now is that I understand his joy. The cost of love is so very worth it! Knowing that my little ones would die so young or knowing that Charles would die at the age of 47, I would have still married him. All of the pain and sorrow was worth the great love we experienced. I still wear the wedding ring he gave me after he found out he was dying. We treasured each and every day, knowing our days were running out. But everyone's days are running out. I didn't realize that until recently, and that every day is amazingly precious. I sometimes observe married couples ignoring each other or being cross over the most trivial offense. What a waste of time! I wonder how often widows and widowers rue the time they wasted with arguments or with cross words—or, perhaps worst of all, by ignoring each other. Thankfully, my wise husband taught me ever so much about love and enjoying marriage—and children.

He also taught me about salvation. He always described himself as a sinner, something I could never see in him. It was very clear to him that he needed a Savior to pay the cost of his sins. His favorite Bible verse was John 3:16: *"For God so loved the world that He gave His only begotten son, that whosoever believeth in him shall not perish but have everlasting life."*

Much of the Bible I still don't understand, but I certainly understood my need for a Savior. I could never reach God's standard of perfection in order to merit heaven, but my Savior, Jesus, has paid my debt for me. How wonderful!

On Christmas Day, our family will all be together for the first time in many, many years. Esther, Nathalie, and Hulda, of course, are here every day. Esther, I suspect is as well as she can be. I will never understand her illness, nor why some days she is morose or upset while on other days she is lucid and talkative and almost giddy. Hulda spends even more time in the barn with the animals and is too shy to talk with anyone but the family. Both Esther and Hulda make too many demands of Nathalie. I can only pray she chooses to marry Ernest and will move on with her life.

Harry and his wife Laura will be coming soon from Minneapolis, where Harry continues his schooling. They have no children yet but will be good parents when little ones begin to arrive. I see Victor every day, but it will be good to have him and Alfhild, his wife, along with their two little girls, Evelyn and Marilyn, filling the house with liveliness. Herbert and Vivian, newly married, live right next door in the old school house that they're remodeling. What would I do without my boys so near? And now I even have the amazing blessing of grandchildren.

And this year dear Ruth is home from her position as principal/teacher in Kettle River. She has brought much joy to the house. She arrived here with a new, beautiful wood stove for the kitchen, as a Christmas gift for the family, and she and Nathalie have been cooking and baking ever since. She even made a big pan of fudge, so delicious it melts in your mouth.

Nathalie and Ruth are thick as thieves. They have such different roles and yet are very close. Ruth, who somehow reminds me of Charles, even handles Esther and Hulda well. I hope she is teaching Nathalie how to do the same. I will be sorry to see Ruth leave after New Year's Day. I don't believe there's been this much laughter in the house for years. And the house really does look nice, decorated with a beautiful spruce tree. It reminds me of the first year we celebrated Christmas in our little house, except instead of the homemade decorations, Ruth brought electric lights, glass balls, and tinsel. It is truly a beautiful sight.

Christmas Day comes and goes with much celebration. I don't believe as many people have ever sat around our large dining room table at one time. Nathalie and Ruth have filled it with wonderful foods: breads, cheeses, sausages, sylta, pickled herring, cookies, cakes, and doughnuts as well as ice cream, raspberry sauce and homemade root beer. I told Nathalie "the table was groaning under the weight of her many creations." She just laughed and then ran off to the kitchen where she had forgotten the doughnuts warming in the oven.

We sit around the table for hours, in no hurry to leave. The little girls are basking in the attention they're receiving. My boys talk about the farm and their "old" mother. They know I can't do much anymore, but seem able and willing to pick up my slack. Finally, Alfhild tells Victor it's time to bring the girls home. I watch admiringly as she bundles up the little ones. She's a good mother. I hold dear Marilyn Ruth as she dresses Evelyn Marie and then reluctantly hand her over to her father.

Victor and Alfhild leave with their children, taking Herbert and Vivian with them to drop off at their home. The rest of us clear the table and begin washing dishes. Harry tells me I look tired, and taking his kind hint, I excuse myself for bed though I'd love to continue listening to the lively conversations.

36

"Time Will Tell"

"Come now, you who say, "Today or tomorrow we will go into such and such a town and spend a year there and trade and get gain;' whereas you do not know about tomorrow. What is your life: For you are a mist that appears for a little time and then vanishes. Instead you ought to say, 'If the LORD wills, we shall live and we will do this or that.' "

James 4:13-15

Another year has come to an end, and 1935 has arrived, ushered in with much fun and festivity. Harry and Laura left yesterday, returning to school. Harry told me he has been offered a teaching position in Crookston, a town in western Minnesota on the Red River Valley that has wonderful farm land. I'm relieved he will not move out of state.

It has been a special treat to have Ruth with us. She brings joy wherever she goes. I ask her if she would consider teaching in Duluth but she simply answers "time will tell."

Now it is the third of January, and Ruth is waiting for her ride with Inez Frasier, her good friend and fellow teacher in Kettle River. Ruth calls to me telling me her ride has arrived. Esther, Hulda, Nathalie, and I scurry to the kitchen to hug Ruth good-bye and to encourage her to come home again soon. We all stand on the back porch, bearing the January cold in order to get a last glimpse of dear Ruth before she returns to her job in Kettle River.

Inez is chatting with Ruth, eager to be on her way in Inez' shiny, new-fangled 1934 Chevrolet passenger car. I have not figured out if the car belongs to Inez or to her mother, who is riding with the girls. Not girls, but young women, well on their way in their careers and obviously in love with life.

The car pulls out of the yard, turning east on the Stark Road. Esther and Hulda go inside to get warm while Nathalie and I stand on the porch, trying to catch just one last glimpse of the car.

Nathalie starts to say something about Ruth but is interrupted by a loud crash. "No, it can't be," I say, trying to deny the fact that a car crash has occurred and that it possibly has involved Ruth. Perspiration runs down my back in the freezing cold. Nathalie pushes me inside as she says she will find out what happened. She goes out the door, bundled in her winter coat, and within the longest hour I've ever lived, Victor and she walk soberly through the door.

I ask Victor why he is here, and he says, "Alfhild was hanging out the wash when she heard the crash. She sent me to see what happened. Nathalie and I arrived at the same time and stayed until the ambulance took Ruth away, but I'm certain she's gone." Esther wraps Nathalie and me in a blanket where we shiver and cry. Within an hour, the sheriff arrives, making it official. The accident occurred when a truck driven by John Granlund hit Inez' car which apparently failed to stop before entering the Midway Road. The impact completely demolished the car and a trailer being pulled by the truck slid into the driveway of the corner gas station, knocking down two gas pumps. Ruth died immediately and Mr. Granlund died shortly after being transported to St. Luke's Hospital in Duluth. Inez, her mother and Mr. Granlund's nineteen-year-old son survived.

Ruth's funeral was held on January 8 at the Augustana Lutheran Church of Midway. The Reverend Harold Peterson conducted a beautiful service. Someone choose neighbors John Stark, Herbert Stark, Clarence Anderson, Allen Backlund and Ed Stark for pallbearers.

And what can I say? My youngest daughter, full of joy, is dead. In a moment she was changed from a sparkling young woman to a mangled corpse. Once again, Charles' theory of the costliness of love has been proven true, and I am at a loss. I pray, I read my Bible, and I feel some comfort, but not enough.

This time I do not even attempt to hide my grief. Ruth's sisters and brothers are saddened just as I am and together we spend hours talking about Ruth, the happiness at Christmas, and the terrible, so unnecessary accident.

My children look to me as if I have answers. I can only tell them that mourning is never easy. I finally think of Charles and tell them his theory of the costliness of love. I remind them that Jesus understands our pain and will walk with us through it. It is strange. Saying the words out loud seem to help all of us, especially me. We sit around the kitchen table, quietly, and then dear Hulda, who seldomly speaks in a group, surprises us all by praying: "Dear God, Ruth is in your hands now just like my kitty cats are. I know you'll take good care of her and the kitties just like my Father told me you would. In Jesus Name, Amen."

And it was enough.

37

A Visit to My Family

> *"So we do not lose heart. Though our outer nature is wasting away, our inner nature is being renewed every day. For this slight momentary affliction is preparing for us an eternal weight of glory beyond all comparison, because we look not to the things that are seen; for the things that are seen are transient, but the things that are unseen are eternal."*
>
> 2 Corinthians 4:16-18

In spite of Ruth's death, spring returns. On Memorial Day, Victor takes me to the cemetery where we place a basket of geraniums and ivy on Charles' grave. We also place pots of flowers on the gravesite of Laurence and Ruth. It hurts me to realize I don't even know where or if Anna, Rosa, and Mary are buried. When they died, deaths of infants were so common that death certificates were not issued, and the graves of infants in cemeteries were not even marked. I can't believe I never thought to ask Charles what had happened to the bodies of our three little girls. I do know the little ones were baptized and am satisfied the children are in the arms of God.

Alfhild has come with us to put a basket on her grandparents' grave. How could life become so twisted? She honors her grandparents while I leave a symbol of my love and sorrow on my husband's and two of our children's graves. We are meant to bury our ancestors--not our offspring. But I can't bear to think of it any more. Instead I look at the blue skies and the budding tree leaves. From somewhere I can smell the first lilac blooms of the season. It is beautiful—even in the cemetery.

I am 66 years old. I'll be 67 in October. I have lived a good life. I was raised by a loving mother and father, and against all odds, married the only man I had ever loved. To my great joy, he also loved me, and we had twenty happy years together that I would not trade for anything. We had eleven children, seven of which reached adulthood. We established the farm Charles desired so much, and we even built the house Charles had promised me. Yes, there were tough times, and we worked hard, but it was all worth it.

I see my boys and how successful they are and I am proud of them. I think of Victor and Alfhild and their two little girls and know they are establishing a good family. They, no doubt will have more children and Herbert and Vivian will start a family, and hopefully so will Harry and Laura.

And I have good girls. Esther and Hulda have their own problems, but they are kind to me, and dear Nathalie is a saint. I truly don't know what I'd do without her.

For me, I am a shell of who I once was. My long hair has turned white and thin, barely covering my scalp. Arthritis has twisted my body, and I am ready to leave this earth at any moment to be with my Savior. Yes, I have made peace with God. I don't understand why he allowed so many of our children to die and for Charles and Ruth to die at such young ages, but someday He will tell me. In the meantime, I remember what Charles said after we'd received a beautiful tapestry from his sister Olivia in Sweden. He told me to look at the underside. "That's how we see our life, as a complicated, disorganization of events, but God sees the other side, a complete, intricate, beautiful pattern that He desires our lives to be."

Oh, yes, God's love and peace are more than enough for me.

Reference Materials

Andersson, Kjell & Per Clemensson, Your Swedish Roots, Ancestry, 2004.

http://zenithcity.com.

Ljungmark, Lars, Swedish Exodus, Swedish Pioneer HistoricaL Society, 1979.

Minnesota Historical Society

Revised Standard Version of The King James Holy Bible.

Sandvik, Glenn, Duluth: An Illustrated History of the Zenith City, Windsor Publications, 1983.

Special thanks to:

Agnetta, a dear cousin who lives in Sweden and generously shared her knowledge of Ljungsjömåla and conditions in Sweden at the time Elina and Charles migrated to America

My four sisters, Evelyn, Marilyn, Jeannie and Sandra who put up with hundreds of questions, shared letters from Sweden and from relatives writing about our family, and offered much encouragement.

Lois and Lindus Lennartson who gave me information about the Esaisson sisters, Amanda and Elina.

Our grown children, Peter for his critiques, Erik for his editing, and Sarah for her enthusiasm.

Finally, and foremost, thanks to my husband Ken for putting up with me when I became caught up in the story I was writing and needed reminders that he would like dinner.

From the Author

What a fascinating two year long process it has been to research the life of my grandparents, Elina and Charles Soderburg. Though a work of fiction, most of the events in this novel are true and have been substantiated. No one seems to know how Elina met Charles, but Elina did live in Ljungsjömåla, a manor house in Blekinge, while Charles, an orphan, was a farmhand all of his adult life in Sweden. Charles did migrate to America first and earned money working on the docks, which he saved to pay for Elina's transportation. There are in existence a collection of beautiful letters written by Elina to Charles, while he waited for her, though the ones in this book were written by me.

I am not certain there was a rift between Elina and Amanda, but I do know, from letters, that Amanda refused Elina's offer to live in their little house after the fire. If, in fact, Amanda had a poor attitude towards Charles, it would be consistent with general attitudes in Sweden when upper class women married beneath themselves.

The overly large emigration trunk not only exists but resides in my home, complete with its key. To me, it is a treasure!

The couple's addresses and home descriptions are accurate. Births and deaths are given as exact as possible. The birth and death of Mary is unsubstantiated in family records, but Mary appears in the 1900 U.S. census as the daughter of Charles and Elina and a death certificate from 1901, listing cause of death as hydrocephalitis, also exists.

Charles' head injury, while working as a laborer on the docks, is a well-established family anecdote as well as being documented in letters written by his son, Harry Soderburg.

LINDA A. HATINEN

Questions remain about the change of the family name from Soderberg, which Charles clearly wrote on his application for citizenship and was recorded on census records through 1930. One theory is that Harry Soderburg's birth certificate was written with "burg", and therefore he adapted that spelling. According to the St. Louis County Office of Records, however, Harry filed a correction to his birth certificate in the 1920's, changing his last name to "Soderburg". Whatever the reason, he eventually convinced his mother and siblings with the exception of my father, Victor Soderberg, to use "his" spelling. Despite confusion at times, I am personally pleased that my father maintained the Swedish spelling "berg" in our last name.

There is no record of how Charles and Elina were able to save money to rent the West Duluth farm, buy the Stark Road land, or for Elina to build their dream house. Mary and Harry Gundersson are figments of my imagination. The purchase and benefit of life insurance is a logical theory, but I have no proof of its existence. If, in fact, Charles and Elina were able to make those purchases, as well as send all of their children to schools following or in place of high school, through only their hard work and savings, the story becomes even "sweeter" to me.

Hulda's and Esther's hospitalizations and circumstances surrounding them are based on hospital records and are a reflection of the poor understanding of mental health issues at the time of the novel and perhaps even now.

Elina Soderburg died on May 4, 1943 at the age of 74. Esther, and Nathalie lived on the farm until their deaths in 1951 and 1974, respectively. Hulda, who moved to a Duluth nursing home when Nathalie became too ill to care for he,r blossomed into a charming, outgoing lady. She died in 1987 at the age of 91. All of the Soderburg women remained single.

Harry and Laura lived near Crookston, Minnesota where Harry taught agriculture. They had no children. Victor, married to his neighbor, Alfhild Stark, continued his poultry farm on the Midway Road until his death in 1968, at the age of 65. He had five children, Evelyn, Marilyn, Carol Jean, Sandra, and Linda.

The Soderburg farm, beautiful and well maintained, still stands on the Stark Road. It is no longer owned by the family nor exists as a functioning farm. The last time I was inside (2017) the wood stove Ruth purchased for her family shortly before her death still stands proudly in the kitchen.

My sister Sandra and her husband live in a beautiful country home on the land Charles and Elina purchased shortly before Charles died. Herbert and his wife Vivian lived in the converted schoolhouse until he died in 1973 at the age of 67. Herbert, as well as working on the Soderburg farm, worked for the railroad and had three children, Ralph, Ruth and Chester. Ruth and Chester now both live in beautiful homes, across the Stark Road from one another, close to their roots.

As I wrote this book, I shed many tears, reliving the family tragedies and trying to imagine how Elina went on with life, especially after losing the love of her life, Charles. Though she died before I was born, the few people who remember her describes her as a hard worker and having a deep faith, which I believe made coping with her losses possible.

I have learned that as I write, I run the risk of missing facts or misinterpreting what I learn and even writing something hurtful. Therefore, I ask forgiveness of anyone I may have offended through my writing. On the other hand, if anyone has been blessed by this novel, I praise God for giving me both the ability and the desire to write. If you have questions and/or comments, feel free to contact me at hattielah48@gmail.com.

I close, appropriately I believe, with the Bible verse etched not only on the Soderburg family gravestone but on the family's hearts as well:

"…..to live is Christ and to die is gain."

Philippians 1:21